THE GERMAN LOTTERY

The Slovenian writer and film-maker Miha Mazzini, born in 1961, is the author of twenty-three books. *The Cartier Project* (1987; US edition, 2004) was ex-Yugoslavia's all-time bestselling novel and was made into a feature film; *Guarding Hanna* (2000; US edition, 2002) was longlisted for the International IMPAC Dublin Literary Award in 2004. He lives in Ljubljana.

Miha Mazzini
THE GERMAN LOTTERY

translated by
Urška Zupanec

$\mathbb{C}$B *editions*

First published in Great Britain in 2012
by CB editions
146 Percy Road London W12 9QL
www.cbeditions.com

The rights of Miha Mazzini and Urška Zupanec to
be identified respectively as author and translator
of this work have been asserted in accordance with
the Copyright, Designs and Patents Act 1988

German Lottery design (opposite and page 49) © Andreja Brulc

Printed in England by Blissetts, London W3 8DH

ISBN 978-0-9567359-3-5

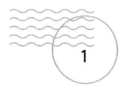

N°. You've got to tell her: no.

I remember how hard it is; you want to scream it, beg with it, but a true *no* is quite ordinary, normal, neither loud nor soft, though there is something in it that comes from your moral core, as I call it. They've dug into you, pushed you, and finally pinned you against your own essence so you can't shrink any further. This is how you say it:

No.

When you say it, that's it. End of story. People feel it. But you've got to be strong inside, you've got to firmly believe, you've got to . . .

Oh, how hard it is!

Until you've said it, can you be a mature and responsible person at all?

It wasn't easy, this *no* of mine. Especially because I had to say it to a woman. For the first and . . . well, actually, also for the last time in my life. Once was enough, that's how strong it was.

Perhaps the time is right for you to hear the story of my success. You're the right age – as old as I was when I became part of the German Lottery.

I'll start telling it when you come to visit me again.

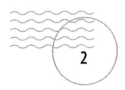

2

They sent me here in the beginning of March 1950 to work at the post office. Youths my age from the home for war orphans were drafted into the army, you had to serve three years back then, but I wasn't accepted because of my bad knee. I was disabled, so they decided I should become a postman.

Yes, I know it sounds strange that someone could look at a young man with a limp and think: he'll make a good postman! But those were different times, socialist times. We were all equal and everyone was qualified for everything. There were no differences. These days it's tougher. You have a limp, you can't be a postman. You have no taste, you can't be a cook. You're impolite and slow, you can't be a waiter. If you start sorting people by their characteristics, there will never be enough of them to fill all the jobs. Someone who is impolite and slow will have to pretend to be polite and quick to get the job, which means he'll be lying to himself and to others. People have a tendency towards the truth and the Yugoslav socialism supported that.

I've wandered a little. I'm sorry.

Back then the post office was in the old building, on this side of the river, right next to the bridge. They pulled it down before you were born. Maybe I could find some pictures . . . I'll have a look fore next time.

It was small, from Austro-Hungarian times. A single counter by the wall, little piles of forms in the corner. A few pens, a bottle of ink, a sponge moistener for stamps, which was always dry, so everybody had to lick their stamps. Later I heard a joke about why President Tito didn't allow his picture to be put on stamps for a long time. Because people would spit on the wrong side. Ha, ha.

Well.

The room was divided down the middle – wood up to waist height and then glass, a window, and behind the window, Mrs . . . well, *Comrade* Leopoldina. We all became comrades at that time and had to use the familiar form of address with each other, which was embarrassing. How could I address this old lady, who must have personally met Emperor Franz Joseph, as Comrade? When I did, she stopped for a moment, as if to check if I were talking to her. Not that we had many dealings. She came in the morning, at eight – we postmen arrived two hours earlier – closed at noon and came back in the afternoon. Good day, good night, that's about all we ever said to each other. I can still see her clearly; she looked like an owl with those glasses of hers.

Like I've said, we postmen arrived at six. The manager stood at the front door checking his watch, so we were always on time. He unlocked the door and we filed in after him. The three of us turned right into the sorting room and he went straight into his office. Lovro and Janez were old postmen, from before the war. Lovro, the poor guy, would immediately sit down at the counter and shake, whining softly. I can still hear his fingers pattering on the counter, just like rain. He didn't sort the mail. How could he? Just before seven, Janez grabbed him by the arm, helped him to his feet, and took him for a walk across the bridge to the pub.

I sorted their mail. They couldn't deal with that too, old and weak as they were. How quick and skilful I was! I even had time to read the newspaper headlines and the captions under the pictures in peace and quiet before they came back.

When they did, half an hour later, I could hardly recognise Lovro, his step sure and self-confident. He often entered the room making fun of me, calling me beanpole and long Monday.

I sorted the mail by delivery, that's what you called it, into a rack, in the same order we put the mail into our bags, which was again the order of our routes.

At half past seven sharp, the manager walked into the sorting room and dragged his finger across the sorted mail. The first time, when I was new, he had to ask me if there was anything special; afterwards he just looked at me and I would shake my head. Lovro and Janez would do the same. I thought the manager looked like a mountain, his finger with the closely-bitten nail like a red hook on white envelopes. Always only the right index finger. He never used his left hand for official purposes, only for smoothing his slightly grizzled hair, shiny with brilliantine.

How softly the envelopes rustled when he bent them. His finger slid and stopped – maybe against a stiffer letter or for no apparent reason – then he drew out an envelope and held it up to the light. Each day he took out a small stack and took it into his office.

A minute to eight, the time for our rounds, he returned the letters, freshly sealed.

The town wasn't big back then. Before I arrived, Lovro and Janez divided it between them. After I started, they took over the new apartment block quarter, here, on this bank, where all the customers were in one place and you didn't need to go from house to house to deliver each letter.

I was left with the old side, or the village side as they called it. Before socialism, the farmers built their houses and stables on the slopes; they didn't want to waste the flat, fertile land. But that was pre-revolutionary, old-fashioned, big-landowner thinking; now they laid concrete and asphalt on the fields.

The houses near the river still huddled together, but those along the slopes were dotted further and further apart. If you take a good look, you'll see the mountains reach towards us like the paws of a cat or a dog. Mail delivery was an endless trudge up and down.

I ate at the People's Kitchen which was built for the factory workers. When I looked down over my delivery route from the highest hill I saw all the rooftops, from under which the smells of cooking climbed up, something different from each house; how confusing and uneconomical, each family making their own meal, while the People's Kitchen served the same to everyone. We were getting communism even in the kitchen!

Postmen should have taken turns in the evening emptying of the mailboxes in the town, but my colleagues had families, so I went back to the post office every evening, took the company bicycle and my bag, and went to collect the mail. When the weather was fine, there was nothing better than a bicycle. What I miss most is the feeling of pushing yourself uphill with your own muscles. The wind, the slope, everything, everything wants to stop you, but you won't give in. Beautiful. How beautiful. Well . . .

I went back to the post office with my bag and sorted the collected mail into four piles: for abroad, other republics, Slovenia, and sometimes for our home town, if necessary. This wasn't often; people still visited each other back then. The manager always came out of his office at eight sharp and went through the piles again. Occasionally, he took a letter or two with him, but less than in the morning, because he knew there would be more managers between him and the addressees, who would try to prevent correspondence between hostile elements.

This is what we did every day, except on Sundays.

That's it.

Have I forgotten anything?

You can yawn away, but I have to explain how the work was organised for you to understand the secret of the German Lottery. If it hadn't been like that, and if the times had been different, it wouldn't have been possible.

Yes . . . one more thing, as I've already started explaining about the times. On the wall there was a picture of Marshal Tito and next to it a large stain where two years earlier Comrade Stalin used to hang. They took him down because he and Tito had a fight. We were all shouting 'Long live Stalin!' and then we suddenly weren't supposed to do it any more, without anybody telling us. After a while it was criminalised, without any law being passed. Those must have been strange times, but they didn't seem so. Probably because of youth, which blinds you somehow. You only see yourself, I think.

Do they teach you any of this in school?

I'll refresh your memory: first Tito and Stalin were friends. Tito was ours and Stalin was the Soviet president. Soviet is what we used to call the Russians back then. They had both quarrelled with the Americans, who isolated Yugoslavia because of it. The borders were closed with the tanks and the army. Then Tito stopped bowing his head to Stalin, and the Soviets isolated us as well. So we had Soviet tanks on our eastern borders and American tanks on our western border. It sounds official, but think about it; the West is right over there, just beyond that hill. The American planes kept flying over our heads. One day our men started shooting and brought one down. Really. We were waiting for the Americans to strike, but nothing happened. They kept flying their planes – they are a superpower after all – but on their side of the hill.

Those were different times . . .

But in spite of the tensions that had continued after the war, I wasn't afraid. I thought we were all in the same boat. Each of us alone, but still in the same boat. Now, I think I've never belonged to something bigger than me, though I've tried. Only when I got mixed up with the German Lottery did I learn about fear. I wasn't just alone, I was unique, separated from the crowd, and with this came responsibility for my actions. A mortifying feeling.

You've got to go already? Stay a little longer. Let me just show you my delivery route.

First, I would stride over the bridge, which seemed big and beautiful. Sometime last year, when I felt my legs

7

wouldn't carry me much longer, I paid for a cab and went to see it. How small and dreary it looked. I didn't even want to leave the car. Maybe it's good that memory and truth go their separate ways sometimes.

Well, over that large and beautiful bridge I went. It had two arches made of concrete; later I saw similar ones in American movies. I was always temped to walk over them like a tightrope walker, but I never dared. Even now, when I think about it, I become nostalgic. You know, I've been thinking about all the things I have to tell you so you'll understand the secret of the German Lottery. Remembering these arches I realised something that may help you, young as you are: memories are about the things you've done, while nostalgia is about the things you haven't done, but should have.

Halfway over the bridge I always looked down at my reflection in the river. Is it still as slow as it used to be? I admit, I was thrilled when I saw the buttons on my postal uniform shine! I didn't linger there long. The bag was full and heavy. I could barely drag it along. I carried it over my right shoulder, so it would weigh down the opposite side of my body, making me limp evenly, or so I thought.

A few days after I started my job, a registered letter arrived addressed to Zora Klemenc, 12 Hero Stane Street. By then, the larger part of the town was named after national heroes who gave their lives for our freedom. That house is gone now; it stood outside the settlement, further up the hill. Not very old, but its grey colour seemed sad to me. Like every house, it had a stack of firewood piled up by its side for the winter, but here the wood was turning rotten and black, as if nobody had used it in several winters. The house had a nice big terrace facing the hill, the woods, and the path that led to the mountains. The blazes had faded by then, but before the war there must have been groups of hikers pouring along it. A little further up the path stood a bunker from the Second World War, but you couldn't see it any longer; the forest was reclaiming the land. The border guards used these paths, but civilians were not allowed to enter the zone.

Well, the letter was addressed to Zora, so I rang the bell. It was one of those bells you had to wind up and release, like an alarm clock.

I was probably still thinking about the firewood, because I was surprised by how scantily clothed she was for the time of the year in that skimpy red dress of hers. Spring was coming and warmth was spreading from noon towards morning and evening, but it hadn't gotten very far yet. The hills were still covered in snow, an icy wind swept down from the mountains, and I felt a shiver under my uniform. There were plenty of poorly dressed people around, but she didn't look poor, though I saw only basic furniture behind her, no luxury.

'Good day, comrade. Are you Zora Klemenc?'
'Yes?'
'A registered letter. Can you prove your identity?'
'Gladly, comrade postman. Just a minute.'

What pride I took in saying those words! A profession doesn't only need a uniform, it needs its own language. Language that sounds strange to the uninitiated, new words that knit us into a community. 'Your identity' – how beautiful it sounds! What does it actually mean?

Zora brought her identity card and held it in front of her

chest. She was really cold, the poor thing, there were goose bumps all over her bare skin, spreading all the way down to the white bra, too small to keep anything except the lower part of her breasts warm.

I took the document and looked carefully at the photograph and then at her. Hair a bit different, the shape of the nose – a strong, proud nose – right, the forehead straight, the lips full and – it occurred to me that she must have pouted too much as a child – somewhat twisty, the chin rounded, the hair dark and curly, the colour of eyes brown in the flesh, but the photograph was in black and white. I also worked out her age, twenty-seven, but she didn't show it.

I gave her the delivery form and showed her where to sign. She had a very loopy signature, twisting to the left.

I gave her the letter.

'Thank you comrade and good day,' I said, starting to turn away.

'Comrade postman?'

She surprised me. I wasn't completely sure of myself in my new job yet. Had I done anything wrong?

'It's cold. Why don't you step in for a drink?'

'No, thank you, comrade. Postmen don't drink on duty. It's against the CP.' I revealed one of our Code of Practice rules to her.

I took leave by touching my peaked cap.

Oh, you're leaving too? OK. Next day, there was another registered letter for Zora. I'll tell you about it next time.

Will you take this cod with you? It's good cold too. They still keep bringing it to me on Fridays, though I've told them a hundred times I don't eat fish.

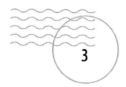

3

How could I have mentioned my mailbag so briefly last time? It means the world to a postman! She's a postman's best friend.

First, defence. Even the most peaceful of dogs go crazy when they lay their eyes on us. Once a St Bernard jumped on my back from the first floor and knocked me to the ground. I didn't know what hit me, but I pushed my bag into its jaws before they snapped.

The owners always say dogs just want to play, and if I had believed that, they would have gnawed me to the bone in my first year. There must be something special about the mailbag, for dogs too. They go after you, but when they bite down on that leather, they don't let go. And you're saved.

There's nothing better than a mailbag beating against your side. In the morning she's heavy, pounding as if she wanted to bring you down, but she gets lighter with each house, and in the end you don't even feel her. Tell me, is there any other job that lets you measure your efficiency so precisely and immediately?

And the smell – what fragrance! Everything is up there, on top of her, the smells of the whole town, the paper, the sweat; but on the bottom, when your nose is alone inside her, there's nature, the cow's udder, fullness and warmth.

They're gone now. Luckily I retired before they introduced the mail trolleys, plastic and wheels. What a shame! Are you a man, or an old lady coming from the market?

Let's leave that. As I've said, the next day there was another registered letter for Zora. I didn't deliver a lot of those as a rule. People were poor, only official letters were sent that way. Courts sent them, for example, and there was also some international mail, from the Red Cross and a similar organisation people contacted about missing relatives.

I must admit, I was glad of every registered letter, because it allowed me to lean on my right leg and rest my left. The first third of my route was OK, but then I started to feel the grinding in my knee, the joint was becoming stiffer and swollen towards the end. At home I cooled it, in the winter just by pressing it against the wall or rubbing it with snow. In the evening, on the bicycle, it didn't bother me at all. Isn't that odd?

Well, she was hanging the washing when I came limping round the corner. I've already told you there was a big terrace between the house and the side of the hill, like a bridge forming flat land where nature afforded none. She was scantily dressed again. Judging by the colour, she was wearing the same dress, only this time I also noticed small white dots. Perhaps it was handed down to her or she got it from an UNRA aid package, because it only reached to her knees. That day was cool and windy, her legs were bare, and she was standing on a footstool to reach the line strung across the terrace.

I said hello by the book and asked for proof of identity. She gave me a surprised look, as if to say, Am I not the same as yesterday? I explained that rules are there to be obeyed.

'All right,' she said and stepped down from the footstool. But she must have leaned on the line too much while doing it, because it came undone and she only just managed to grab it.

'Help! Hold it!'

I took the line, but most of the washing was already folding along the ground.

'Pull it up! Pull it up!'

I lifted my arms high up and the washing started flapping again.

She brought her hands before her mouth.

'Oh, thank you. You've spared me from doing the washing again in that icy creek!'

My arms started to shake. 'Comrade, please, could you fasten the line?'

'Of course!'

She grabbed the free end and wanted to pull it to the hook around which it had been fastened before.

'Come closer!'

I took a few steps so I stood right next to her. She quickly made a knot but couldn't reach to put it over the hook.

'Closer, closer!'

I was pushing closer and closer to her, but it didn't help.

She quickly went to get the footstool. Now we were face to face. My arms started jerking and going numb from the strain.

She stopped right before my face, as if she had just noticed something.

'How strong you are,' she whispered, and I felt her breath

on my skin. It smelled of coffee – real coffee, not chicory. And then there was that strange, heady scent – perfume – which made me dizzy, so I started to breathe heavily.

The other day I was listening to a TV programme about the sort of things they put into perfumes; that can't be healthy.

Anyway . . . We kept pressing and pressing against each other, but we still couldn't reach the hook. My legs became shaky, the bag was still quite heavy, my knee started playing up, sweat began trickling down my back; I felt it between my shoulder blades.

She placed her arms around my neck, turned me around, and tried to fasten the line to the hook leaning over me. She wasn't very good at it, but it wasn't the right moment to point that out. Some women just aren't cut out for some things, but they're offended if you mention it. Everyone is blind to his own faults. What can you do?

In her effort, she leaned on me with all her weight, and I really couldn't bear it any more. I yielded, she screamed, and the washing swished down again. I quickly got up and held it up again.

'The bag. Come on, let me take your bag!'

She tried to pick it up by the strap, but she couldn't, so she got up on the footstool again, on tiptoe, and then she tried to lift the strap slowly over my head. She was also sweating under her armpits. I saw a drop trickle into her cleavage, and the tips of her bra – they were very pointy back then – were rubbing through that flimsy dress against the heavy cloth of my uniform. She lifted the strap, as much as she could. I had to bow my head and found myself in her cleavage; what a wonderful scent. I kept opening

14

my mouth, gasping. She moved away. The cold air did me good. She was there before me with the bag, which was too heavy for her, dragging it along the ground.

'Comrade, be careful with the bag!'

'Yes, of course.' She put it on the table and got back on the footstool. Again she leaned over me, again I breathed heavily from the perfume, and then . . . I'm embarrassed to say this. I know you're very loose nowadays, but I'm old school. It came on so fast, I had to remind myself I was a state official on duty. I was filled with strange emotions.

I wanted to tell you this the way we always tell stories, as if we were the main characters and had everything under control. But I'm too old to fool around, so I'll tell it like it was.

Strange feelings, I said. Words are so lifeless sometimes! Not that I'd never had those kinds of feelings before, but this time they were so strong and powerful I was becoming afraid of myself. My eyes were darting, flitting, searching for anything to turn to while my body was trapped in her domain. I tried thinking about the bag, wondering if it was safe. I watched it on the table. Was it just as full as before? Did someone pinch a letter from it? – a lost letter, a postman's greatest nightmare. That was all I thought about, and about the Code of Practice. I kept saying it silently like a prayer, like Hail Marys and Lord's Prayers, saying she was a customer and I an official delivering registered mail. The procedure might have got a little out of hand, but everything would soon be back to normal. I just had to hold out.

It felt like eternity. Zora was trying, but clumsy as she was, it took her forever until she finally managed to slip the line on the hook and rescue the washing.

We were facing each other, completely soaked.

'Thank you!'

I nodded. 'Comrade, a postman is always ready to help.'

'That's nice to hear.'

I straightened my uniform and put the bag over my shoulder.

'Do you come round in the evenings too?'

'No, delivery is only in the mornings. But if you drop off your mail in a mailbox by 7 p.m., it's collected the same day, except on Saturdays when you have to drop it off by 1 p.m.'

She gave me a stunned look. There was something so strange in her gaze that I just stood there, unable to move.

She was examining me, I thought, like a puzzle. Then there was a flicker in her eyes and she nodded and turned away.

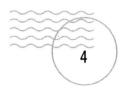

4

I know, I know. You're giving me the same funny look. But these are different times, really different. When I was a kid, I never wondered what I would be when I grew up. You have so many choices nowadays. You are offered all kinds of things. I hear you only need to make a wish and it comes true. I was born before these wishes, when it was completely clear I would stay at home and look after my parents. Who else would? My six brothers were already grown up or almost grown up, tall, shapely men, while I was just a lanky beanpole. Late crop they called me. One of those born after a woman's time has passed. Or that's what the future parents think, and she doesn't find it strange when that time of the month just won't and won't come, while her belly swells, so in the end I arrive.

It was clear the oldest one would inherit the farm, the others would leave home, and I would stay on to help my parents and take care of them. A shepherd and a farmhand. I could never imagine my father to be helpless, though. We were tall, after our mother, while he was a stocky, stout man who could lift a log by himself. He was a good father who brought food to the table and left me alone. But my brothers didn't. We stayed out of each other's way, but when our ways crossed they would kick me or slap me, whichever was more convenient. That's why I liked cats and dogs; if they got in my brothers' way before me, they took the beating and I could slip away.

Mother was really kind-hearted; she had a heart of gold. After I was born, she had trouble walking and spent most of her days in bed, often moaning. How she took care of me! Wonderfully! She would watch me and shake her head: 'How will you ever survive, puny as you are? How?' Later her worries spread to everything. She was reading the Bible more and more and told me about saints and their suffering, about dying. Sainthood is a job that demands the whole person. On the one hand, I liked listening to her, as she strung out her words softly and gently, looking me in the eye and telling me we were all doomed, the world would end in fire, the end was drawing near. Then she stopped and waited. Spoke . . . waited . . .

Ha, that's funny. You know what I thought of after all these years? How I liked to hide away under the branches of a weeping willow that reached down to the ground and covered me. I liked being alone most of all. I was happiest when they left me alone, forgotten and hidden away. I sat on a root and looked into the water. Picked up a stone and threw it. Plop, it went through the surface and the circles went out, out, slowly . . .

Well, it was like that. That's how she threw each story into me. Like a stone. And then she watched the circles of feelings that spread in my eyes. Funny, isn't it?

Like I said: I liked being alone most of all. I was waiting under the willow tree for Moses to come floating by in a little basket and put an end to all my fears and worries; he would guide me and I would be safe. I know I got everything mixed up. I was a child. If baby Moses had come, I would have had to look after him in the end!

I would often huddle with the cows I tended. Their smell, radiating warmth, beautiful. Alone. I also liked bringing water in the morning and warming it up for breakfast, before everybody woke up, before the day dawned. And so one morning, a year before the end of the war, I was standing on the river bank, getting water, looking down at the valley. The sky in the west was still pitch black, while in the east the first streaks of light began to spill out. There was a straight line among them, and at first I didn't notice it was coming my way. Then I heard droning, roaring, more droning, rattling, silence, silence. A plane, getting closer, gliding and leaving bands of smoke behind it. Something began to open underneath it – parachutes. They jumped, and I watched them sway down to the valley, to the town. The plane kept coming at me, lower and lower. I couldn't take my eyes off it. It was getting closer and larger, there was fire in the cockpit. The plane went over me and I remember the feeling – was it a feeling of terror or beauty or both? – a burning plane, metal plates falling off, fire hissing out of its cracks and windows, a burning cross, a cross coming down from the sky. My mother had been right, the world was coming to an end. A cross of fire, black on the outside and glowing within, was coming. 'Jesus,' I said. Jesus was all I could gasp as the cross went over me, and I felt its heat, got licked by its flames, wrapped by the smoke, while the air swelled and spawned swirls as it went over me . . .

And this is all I remember.

It crashed on our farm and killed everyone, including the cows. One tiny shred hit me, and I've carried it in my knee till this day. Back then, they didn't know how to get it out, later I wouldn't let them, and now I'm too old for surgery.

Like I've said, everything disappeared.

Even what I was to become when I grew up.

First, I wasn't conscious. I was lying in the hospital, my knee was festering. It healed only after the war had ended. They put me into the home for war orphans, and there I met a teacher who was the first to tell me that the stories about saints and the end of the world were just old wives' tales. This is what he said:

'Saints, you say? It's true, they did die for their beliefs. But what beliefs? That a virgin gave birth? That you could feed thousands of people with a single fish? That we were made out of clay and breath, and women out of a rib? That someone travelled inside a whale? That . . . Would you die for something like that? Isn't it better to die for equality, egalitarianism, for prosperity of all people, for communism, which is coming? A man has to see the truth and accept it instead of blinding himself with lies. How can he see the truth about exploiters, if he believes in fairytales?'

He also asked himself how a blinded man could freely elect the best representatives of the people and answered that the elections must not offer any choice until superstitions had been rooted out and the eyes of the people opened.

On the one hand, I felt terrible because he was indirectly saying bad things about my deceased mother, but on the other hand . . . I would say he was right even today. He was an old communist, there from the very beginning. In the war, he joined the partisans and was badly hurt. That's why they made him a teacher. How I looked up to him, like he was a God! I took in everything he said, gaping. Every word was precious.

He personally knew the seven secretaries of SKOJ and told us stories about them all the time.

They don't teach you about that any more, do they?

I thought so.

Well, SKOJ was an organisation of young Yugoslav socialists. First you were a SKOJ, then you became a communist. Their leader was called a secretary. There were seven of them, one after the other, a very dangerous job. They were all killed in different ways, from executions to torture in jail. They were true martyrs, but not like the ones my mother talked about who were meant to scare children; these were meant to encourage people on their way to a bright future.

I read books about them and imagined I was also as brave and determined as they were. It can't be hard to die, once you're filled with faith and believe that what you're doing is the right thing to do.

Everything is easy, if it's meaningful. At your age, you must wonder a lot about the Big Meaning: life, God, purpose? We're not made to be just lost mail. There has to be a sender and an addressee.

They told me I wasn't cut out to be a soldier, but I would make a good postman. So I got my job. It was so much easier in those days. Before socialism, your parents told you what to do; after socialism, the state did. You were never left to your own devices. You didn't have to think about it. There were rules for everything, a clear order. If somebody died, you knew how to give your condolences. At a birth, you knew how to congratulate. And now you have to find your own way, without any rules. People aren't made for that much decision-making and thinking!

They said: you're a postman.

And I was.

I got the CP, a little booklet titled Code of Practice. Everyone got them, soldiers too. Every job had its rules. I got my uniform, cap and bag. I learned the booklet by heart. It had rules for every possible situation. Registered letter: what I say, what they say. A letter with insufficient stamps. A letter with an incomplete address. Everything. I knew it by heart and felt safe. If we all stick to the rules, then we all act the same, which means we're all the same. And we all know what we can expect. We are all safe.

I was a postman entering life, and I had everything under control.

And then Zora's line broke.

That wasn't in the CP. No. I knew I shouldn't give my bag to an unauthorised person, but how could I resist? The fate of the washing was in my hands. One of the rules said I had to look after the reputation of my profession in public. I didn't break that rule.

Although . . . Did she notice my embarrassment?

The secretaries of SKOJ were not married, they didn't even have girlfriends. They worked and died for the party alone. I'm embarrassed to talk about this, but I have to, so you'll understand how different those times were. Nowadays, you watch porn and sex on TV or on your computers. We had that on farms too, the only difference was that we watched the animals. But we didn't know anything about what couples did when they weren't having sex. When I think about it, maybe it's not that different now.

Anyway, my parents surely didn't have sex any more, but they didn't have anything else either. They lived together, saw each other at mealtimes, each on their side of the table. When you have to work a lot, it can't be any other way. And little children are like puppies. They learn by copying, not by listening, because they don't understand the words.

That night, I found it so hard to fall asleep. I was tossing and turning, but not as much as I might have, had I not been afraid one of the neighbours might complain. They gave me a small room in the first apartment block they built for the workers of the new factory. I could hardly believe I had the whole room to myself. It was small, but I was the only person in it! Later they named these apartments 'homes for singles' and put two or three of them in each room.

I was turning slowly, like meat on a spit. The bed was creaking. I was looking at the ceiling, at the reflection of the street lamp. I relived all the feelings of our encounter; they started twisting and growing more and more confusing.

'CP, CP,' I was whispering and obviously fell asleep, because Zora appeared before me with a mailbag in her hands. What a beauty! Not like my old bag, but a brand new, shiny bag. I started going towards it, reached out, and suddenly held Zora in my arms. I felt her skin through the light fabric of her dress. The bag had disappeared. I jumped up, startled, and went to get washed up. Luckily the others were fast asleep. Nobody saw me as I felt my way into the shared bathroom at the end of the hallway, because I didn't even dare to switch on the light.

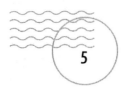

5

In the morning, something strange happened. It was still dark and cold. I was hurrying to the post office, when I suddenly stopped and started staring into the manhole of the town sewer. The round cover had caved in and only the rim was left behind; the roadmen didn't put up a danger sign. Some poor soul could have broken something. I prodded it with my leg, rubbed against the rim; it didn't give. I wondered why I was standing there, looking at something totally unimportant – something that was none of my business – with the concentration, attention and sharpness that you'd expect if the thing were screaming at me.

I've got to leave. I've got to get to work! The rules said I mustn't be late.

Somehow I managed to pull myself away, and the first thing I saw at the office was the wastebasket. Actually, its rim, the circle.

Circle?

I could barely concentrate to sort the mail, and the pattering of Lovro's fingers bothered me more than usual.

Fingers, finger.

Circle, ring.

A dim glow under the light.

The wedding ring.

The hand signing for the registered letter.

The hand stretching the line above me.

Yesterday, Zora wasn't wearing her wedding ring, but the day before she was.

She's married.

At that moment, I pulled out a new registered letter for her from the pile.

You've got to leave, already? OK, till next time, then.

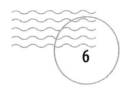

6

What's this, then? Waste service? You're right to cancel it, so careful; you'll do well. Where do I sign? Here? That's impossible. So many copies? Have the garbage men gone crazy?

Thank you. You're a good boy, you are.

Where was I?

There was another registered letter for Zora. Though I shouldn't have delayed the work process, according to the rules, I had a good look at it. It was sent from the neighbouring town. The address was written in capital letters, in a woman's hand, I'd say. I tried to think of the previous envelopes. Wasn't only the first one in a different hand?

I was tempted to read what it said. I admit, when my colleagues went for a walk, I held it up to the light and looked hard. I used to be hawk-eyed and now I'm mole-eyed.

A single sheet, folded. A gentle hand must have been at work, probably in pencil, because I didn't notice any suggestion of typewritten words or ink.

I was embarrassed over my non-postmanlike behaviour! Working less than three weeks in the calling of my life and already on the brink of breaking the rules.

I didn't expect my job to be a role, but a way of living.

Not pretending, but being. During my career, I met women in my delivery rounds who were expecting marriage in the same way. Something that would put an end to all their worries – salvation, happiness, surrender. No more uncertainties of a single girl; from the 'yes' moment on, the rules would be clear. Now I remember, I've already told you about this. Well, my postal rules were clear to me only the first couple of weeks. By the third week, they were already becoming muddled. And that was only the beginning.

I'll tell you all about it. There's something else you see a lot as a postman. Deathbed confessions. Some patients tell the truth regardless of the consequences. We must have the love for truth in us, that moral core – how I repeat myself – the essence that remains in the end when life has gnawed us down.

I see you're impatient. Yes, yes, you've got to go and sort out these papers, I understand.

I checked Zora's identity and delivered the letter.

She invited me in for a drink.

That was when I broke the rules for the first time. Curiosity killed the CP booklet. And I wanted to know, of course, to learn the truth. My whole life has been one big struggle for the truth. Well, and the weather was also bad. I was getting drenched through my raincoat. I was cold, while an inviting warmth was coming from her and from behind her.

But I sat down on the very edge of the chair, barely touching it, clasping my bag firmly. I'd never let it go again.

She wasn't wearing her wedding ring.

She poured drinks. I kept looking at the ring finger of her left hand. I thought I saw a trace.

I took the glass, tasted the drink with my tongue, sweet and tempting, I drank it and started to feel the burn.

'Another one?'

I shook my head.

Stared at the finger.

She noticed and rubbed her skin as if she wanted to rub off the evidence.

We sat on opposite sides of the table in a small room that looked more like a roofed appendage of the terrace. A table, cupboard, two chairs, a vase of catkins, an old radio. In the corner, a clothes stand with prongs forming a crown on top. A hat was stuck on one of them, and a walking stick was propped against the base of the stand.

'You're married.' I looked her in the eye.

She stopped short in the middle of a deep breath. She nodded.

'It's not right.'

She was still nodding.

We were silent.

'They came for him, comrades in long black leather coats, at dawn, two years ago. I still keep waking up at that time and can't go back to sleep. I don't know where he is.'

My eyes wandered to the letter I had just delivered. It lay on the table.

Silence.

'I've got to go,' I said, but remained seated.

Her eyes grew rounder and rounder until big tears started trickling from them, like from a flooded well; they ran down her cheeks, wetted her collar. She bit her lower lip; her nose wrinkled and her face started to twist.

I felt as if a hand were squeezing my heart. I couldn't breathe.

Code of Practice!

At that moment I realised why codes and rules are so good. Because they allow us to act, even in situations that would otherwise make us lose our heads and drag us down with them.

'Delivery is waiting.'

I ran out the door, still clasping my bag. I had a disgusting, burning sweet taste in my mouth.

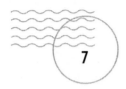

Zora didn't get any more registered letters after that, which was a big relief. She didn't get any other mail either, so I could hurry by her place with a bowed head as quickly as my leg allowed. The gravel crunched under my soles, betraying my presence, so I hurried even more and made even more noise. In the end, I was practically skipping and had to rest by the bunker, sometimes for a few minutes at a time, before I could catch my breath and move downhill, to the small settlement in the side valley.

I don't remember the first time I sat down in the garden of comrades Marija and Ivan, both pensioners. I'm sure I never had a registered letter for them. They spent all nice days in their garden; only when it rained did I see them each in a separate window. She watched her flowers sadly, and he watched the clouds, moving his mouth as if he were eating them in his mind. In rainy weather, we would just wave at each other, but otherwise I would always sit down, for a little while at least, on the chair that was already waiting for me.

Ivan shines right out in my memory; he comes forth as if being born, bald head first. He often bowed his head, shook it silently, then raised it, smiled, and winked at me. First, I was embarrassed, because I thought it had to do with my turning down the liquor, but then I realised he was winking all the time. Not often, but suddenly and violently. It never happened when he was looking at his wife, though.

Marija used to perch like a pigeon; she kept sinking for a while after her behind touched the chair. I wouldn't say she was fat, but she must have been soft, because her body shrank, and little rolls started popping out from it one after another, wobbling slightly when she spoke.

I don't remember what we talked about. Probably the weather. There's always the weather. They didn't have any children, and I got the feeling they didn't need any. Their eye contact was enough for them. I never stayed very long. Partly because of the job, but mostly because I started feeling like a third wheel. As if they had a precise amount of attention for me each time, and when I used it up, their eyes would become fixed on each other for longer and longer periods of time, and it was time for me to get going.

It sounds mean, but it wasn't. They were self-sufficient and didn't need anyone or anything. Those five or ten minutes a day were their gift to me, and that's how I took it. I envied them their peace and contentment and hoped one becomes like them with age. It's not true, not at all, I can tell you now from my experience. I wished to be a part of their peace. No, that isn't quite right. I wished I had come from that kind of peace – that their home had been my home, and I a child in it. I have a feeling that, in addition to the memories of our homes, we also have memories of the way our homes should have been, and the difference fills us with anger and unrest. I envied Marija and Ivan, but for me that stop was also a precious safe haven from the busy world. And besides, their house was almost right in the middle of my delivery route and my knee needed a rest.

The spring was in full bloom, and it was getting warm for the time of the year. I started sleeping with my window open and was sometimes awakened by the shooting in the mountains. I had a feeling the whole town tightened, waiting for the artillery, the aeroplanes, but as the shooting died down, we went back to sleep. The aggression of the imperialist West had not begun; it was just our border guards shooting at a defector or a spy they spotted. Once I saw comrades in long black leather coats bringing from the forest three bodies wrapped in sheets and loading them onto a truck. When I wanted to walk past, they pulled out their guns, then stopped as I saluted, returning the salutation and waiting motionless until I disappeared around the bend.

The factory was already beginning to run. Its formal opening was announced. The apartment block was filling up with workers brought from all over Yugoslavia, and I heard all kinds of languages. I didn't even know there were so many. Among the old wives' tales and Bible stories my mother used to tell me, I realized there might be a true one about Babel. Letters started arriving with addresses written in strange, angular letters. The first one seemed so suspicious that I showed it to the manager, who only smiled and came back with a piece of paper on which their alphabet and our letters, all belonging to the same country, were printed together, next to each other, so I could check what was what. I learned quickly and sorted the letters correctly. It wasn't hard. The strange writing and names belonged in my colleagues' delivery routes.

In a few days . . . No, no, no. It wasn't a few days. It

must have been longer. Weeks? I don't know. Well, it's not important. I only remember the Poles seized all the Church property. When I read the headline in the papers, I couldn't imagine what the communists would do with all those churches. What would my mother have said? Well, that I knew.

I wasn't rushing by Zora's house any more, and when I dared to glance towards the terrace, I saw men's shoes. A fresh coat of polish, shined. Above them, two legs in trousers, pressed, and before I could stop myself I was staring at Nikolaj. He was sitting and looking at me. There were some books piled next to him, and some sheets of paper before him; he was writing. And looking at me. The wind swept down from the mountain, the sheets stirred, and he clapped them down with his hand, like an irritating fly.

Slap.

'No mail, comrade,' I stuttered.

He nodded, and the metal rims of his glasses shined. Comrade; how unsuitable it seemed for him. He looked like a gentleman, a young teacher from before the war. Narrow moustache, pallor, hair straightened with brilliantine, tie done up exactly in the middle. Eyes a bit too close together, skin too pale, almost transparent on the temples.

The post office manager must have been such a gentleman when he was young, but Nikolaj took up much less space, slender as he was. However, there was something about him, which I noticed later in my delivery rounds. Some slight people created a feeling of space around them, as if they took up more of it than actually belonged to them. I can't explain it, really. That's what he was like. He was sitting, I was standing, he was smaller than me anyway,

33

but now that I look at him in my mind's eye, it feels as if I'm looking up at him, which surely can't be right. As if memories are made each time anew – when we evoke them – from what has been, what we wish had been, and who we are at the given moment.

Of course, I didn't know then what his name was. But it occurred to me that Zora's husband had returned and, yes, he was wearing a ring.

'Young man, I'm not expecting anything.'

He wasn't much older than me – twenty-five, as I learned later – but compared to him, I seemed like a boy. There was something serious and experienced in his face – knowledge, probably from the books – and at the same time there was no trace of fear as in the faces of others who had returned from prisons. I met a lot of them in my rounds. They jumped up at the sound of the bell, sent their wives to get the door, and signed reluctantly. Nikolaj took off his glasses and held them up to the sun. He examined the lenses carefully and blew away a speck of dust.

'I like to see perfectly,' he said.

I didn't know what to do.

'Sit down, young man. Have a rest,' he offered. I didn't know if I liked the way he addressed me, but I had to accept it. After all, he used a kind expression for a village beanpole, a shepherd, I thought as I observed his noble bearing and modest but tidy suit. It couldn't have been very expensive, but he wore it as if it had been. Which gave him the air – well, I've told you already.

I was clasping my bag against my chest, sitting on the edge of the chair. I caught myself staring at the ground, so I looked away. I saw the tight washing line, the knot on its end where Zora and I . . . his wife . . . in his absence. I felt my ears flush and my cheeks tingle. I was turning bright red, though the sun had only just come up from behind the mountains.

I quickly turned to him, though I didn't dare look him in the eye.

A Cloud in Trousers it said on the cover of the book on the top.

I shuddered. Is he hinting at the feelings I had while holding the washing line? They were really turbulent, as if clouds were gathering and building up into a storm. Is he trying to hint he knows everything? Has Zora told him? Has she begged his forgiveness in tears? Has she repented? Should I do the same?

There were some more books in the pile, and the bottom one was turned so I could read what was written on its spine: Dostoyevsky, *Crime and Punishment*. Law books? Russian! I had heard terrible things about Soviet processes – no mercy . . .

I was growing stiff with fear.

Nikolaj let me suffer.

The door opened, and Zora brought two cups of coffee on a tray and placed them before us. She didn't even look at me. I saw with the corner of my eye that she was wearing warmer clothes. She caressed her husband's shoulder and went back into the house.

She was wearing the ring again.

We didn't have the money for coffee back home; we drank chicory. We didn't get it in the home for war orphans either. But here . . . At first it didn't occur to me that the coffee was for me, even though it was steaming under my nose and smelled just as heady as Zora's perfume, though very different.

A new wave of blushing.

Nikolaj offered me a cigarette. I turned it down. My brothers' smoking used to make me cough, so I never even tried it.

I averted my eyes to the cup. Stared at the black surface, which grew calm and clear. It reflected a cloud in the sky in its dark way.

I heard Nikolaj pick up his cup and take a sip. After he swallowed, he let out a deep sigh and hummed.

I brought up my hand with a feeling of reaching out for something which was not meant for me, that it was too good for me, that I was pretending, faking, lying, cheating, that they would find me out and laugh at me. But then I remembered we had socialism, we were all equal, and coffee was for everyone, though they couldn't get it in the shop and had to buy it on the black market.

I had a sip. It was hot and I burned my mouth; I wanted to spit it out, but I controlled myself, because it was too expensive. I secretly cooled it by blowing. I wouldn't give up.

'Young man, I'd like to ask you something.'

The coffee went down the wrong way.

I waited without raising my face. He was silent until I gathered up the strength to look at him.

His eyes surprised me, looking at me softly and gently.

'Young man, have you done any good deeds today?'

'Eh?'

'Good deeds?'

I frowned while thinking about it. Look, I'm frowning even now, while telling you about it.

'What do you mean?'

'A good deed. Have you done something you didn't have to and helped your fellow man with it?'

He was asking me about complicated things. I had to think about it. I understood what he wanted to find out, but not why. I took a few more sips. The smell captivated me, but I didn't like the taste. Even today, the most unbelievable thing about coffee for me is the difference between its inviting smell that crawls up your nose and the taste which awaits you in the mouth.

'I've delivered the mail,' I said.

'This is your regular work, not a good deed.'

'One lady got a letter from the Red Cross.'

He waited for an explanation.

'I know from the weight of the forms in the envelope whether it's good or bad news.'

'Oh, I see. However, young man, you get paid for your work and you follow your code of practice.'

I agreed. I emptied the cup but wouldn't let go of it. What would I do with my hands otherwise?

'A good deed is above codes and rules. Sometimes it even goes against them. Have you done anything like that? Today? Yesterday? A week ago?'

I blushed again and couldn't help myself; I looked at the line above us.

'Young man, think about it and tell me tomorrow.'

It took me a while before I realised I could leave.

I never drank coffee again. It's really not for me. What hell it gave me – the runs! Luckily my route was near the forest, so I could run into the bushes.

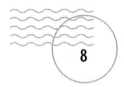

8

Have you done any good deeds today? Yesterday? Well, when you start thinking about it, you quickly ask yourself, hey, what is a good deed anyway? There's a babbler inside us that always distracts us when we want to get to the truth. It twists our words, and every way it twists them, they sound right. It finds a reason and explanation for everything. Words are like drills; you can keep twisting them until you drill a hole into anything. But suddenly you realise you're not the one doing the twisting; the words start twisting you.

However, our moral core knows what good deeds are and knows if we do them or not. It is immovable and independent of words.

Anyway, I couldn't think of a single good deed. Had I helped an old lady cross the road? I had! But that was being polite, following one of the rules in the Code of Practice, in the etiquette part. I thought about the seven secretaries of SKOJ. Was it possible to do a good deed and stay alive?

I soon caught myself thinking how to avoid running into Zora's husband. Change my route, so their house would not be on it? But it stood right between the little settlements. I'd have to pass it anyway, unless I went high up into the mountains, into the border guards' territory, which I was afraid of.

But on the other hand, he was a civilian, and I was an official! In uniform! I got up and went to the wardrobe. I carried my jacket to the window and let the buttons and the epaulettes shine in the dim glow. This is me, a postman. My uniform is my armour! I've got a cap with a peak, the Code of Practice in my pocket. He hasn't got anything. A civilian is nothing but a newborn baby – dirty, wet and naked – without a uniform, without work, without a purpose or a goal!

I fell asleep with my cap on.

When Zora brought two coffees, I declined.

'Not for me, thank you.'

How simple! Listen again:

'Not for me, thank you.'

My first *no*. The first step to the *no* I had to say at the end of the story about the German Lottery.

It worked. Nikolaj gestured to Zora to sit down with us. She drank the coffee herself and smoked a cigarette while sipping it. I thought her smoking was good, socialist. Before the war, women with cigarettes were frowned upon, but now they were proving we were all equal.

I released the pressure of my bag against my chest just a tiny little bit, because the clasp was digging into my collarbone. Filled with courage, I raised my head and looked at them. I couldn't read Zora's face, but Nikolaj was gazing at me with kind and gentle eyes.

'Let's make the introductions,' he said.

And we did.

We nodded and shook hands, raising ourselves a bit. The chairs creaked, the coffee smelled sweet. Those were easy minutes, like they always are when you know what to do and how to do it. Etiquette was invented just for that, I tell you.

Finally we arrived at the subject of good deeds again, and my strong will dissolved.

It didn't do any good, clasping my bag with my right hand, sliding my left hand over my peaked cap, watching my shiny buttons, trying to catch a whiff of the leather and of my uniform; the smell of the coffee was louder and more intrusive.

'I understand,' Nikolaj said, caressing his books. 'I understand. I'd like to put your mind at ease. Listen . . . I was absent for some time . . . I've had time to think . . . I've realised that the world lacks good deeds. People are bitter, angry, sad. All the wars, all the suffering. The First World War, the economic crisis, the Second World War, our fratricidal war, the Informbiro and the present crisis, atom bombs, the third world war that could start any moment on these borders, the crossroads of the East and the West, two hostile systems . . . How can an ordinary man who only wants peace and prosperity bear all these terrible pressures? Tell me, do you think people are happy and satisfied?'

I shook my head.

They were still waiting for me to say it:

'No.'

At first it came out muffled, so I cleared my throat and said it again.

'Do they accept their mail with a smile? Do they chat with you?'

I shook my head.

They waited.

'Some set their dogs . . .' I began carefully, and then things started pouring out. I was surprised at myself. In the evenings, I sometimes relived the things that were now gushing out of me. I recalled them, one by one, sometimes only fragments, but now they were joined into a sticky chain, and when I spat the first piece out, all the others came out with it, and I couldn't bite through them:

'One man keeps a dog on a chain. There's only half a metre between the dog and the wall, and he wants me to come up to him through there and deliver his mail personally. I get all wet from the dog's slobber. Another one puts down the time of my arrival every day and nags me about every minute. There's a woman who sets her sons against me, and they set the dogs . . . One comrade sawed every stair in her staircase and wants me to come up to her. Another nailed an extra plank on her doorframe, though I bumped my head into her doorframe even before . . .'

I ran out of breath.

Nikolaj nodded.

'You see?' he said. 'You see? The state of mankind. Let's say those people are evil, and we can't help those. Perhaps you are born evil. Maybe you grow evil, but when you go down that road, you can perhaps come back only by yourself. There's nothing we can do. But what about those who became evil because of poverty? As long as you starve, your brain thinks only of your stomach, it doesn't think about anything else but filling up its brother the belly. When was human individuality born? In prehistoric times, everybody was equal, everybody was living in communism! Everybody was doing and thinking the same things. But then somebody had the first secret! And this secret is what made him different from the others. A secret builds a man from the inside. But the problem with secrets is you can't see them. You look at a horde of prehistoric people, and you can't tell who's got a secret and who hasn't. It was out of historical necessity that an individual was also formed on the outside – and only material goods can do this. Wealth! This is the only thing that shows! The true individual man, the true man of Western civilisation is one who is rich on the outside and has secrets on the inside. Do you agree?'

I didn't understand anything, but I was a bit scared that all the talk about secrets might be against the law.

He didn't wait for my answer.

'The will to power is first of all the will to a secret, to wisdom, to gathering knowledge and words inside you. Every piece of information I know and someone else doesn't is one secret more for me! My advantage, my point! Take a look at these books. Take a look!'

He was touching them like piano keys, using all his fingers.

'The first stage. But when you're sated on the inside, the will to power pushes you on, to the outside. You have to balance both to fulfil your natural potential. And so you acquire the riches. Do you follow?'

The only thing I noticed was that he had stopped addressing me formally.

'Errr,' I stuttered.

Zora patted him on the shoulder and whispered something in his ear.

'You're right, as usual.' He nodded to her and lit another cigarette, though the last one was still burning in the ashtray.

42

'Where was I? Ah, what a history this little country has had in such a short time. How many families in which the children killed each other – some collaborators, the others partisans. Horrible. What a century! The bloodiest ever; and we won this accolade despite our ancestors' utmost efforts in cruelty and killings. You're a postman. You know everything and everyone; nothing gets past you. How many of these people are there among your customers?'

'Well, the old ladies . . . comrades. Widows and widowers . . .' I knew all the people on my route: images of houses and faces went through my mind.

'Zora, would you . . .' said Nikolaj, and his wife slowly handed him a stack of little coupons. Slowly, like a card player, he laid them down on the table, one next to the other.

Food stamps.

Oh, that reminds me, you couldn't just buy food in a store back then. You needed to have special coupons, which said what you could get and how much of it.

Nikolaj turned to Zora and waited for an explanation.

'My father . . . is a general. He has given me up, because I married a poet and a writer . . .'

She quickly stroked his shoulder.

'And also because – well, the two-year absence. But my mother, she keeps sending me the food stamps, secretly. I don't want them, we can get by. We are modest. So –'

Her husband took over:

'We want to give these ten food stamps to the ten neediest people in town. It's too small a gift to help families with many children, and they get food stamps from the government anyway. But nobody helps the lonely widows who lost everything, as if they could live on air. That's why we've thought of you. Please excuse me for being so direct. Thank you. You're a postman. You know your delivery route. I don't want to be personal, but you seem like . . . a good man. I'd just like to ask you to take the food stamps and give them to the right people on your route.'

I leaned forward. I couldn't believe it. I was confused. I'd never met that kind of people before. They wanted to give away, to someone else, something they could use themselves?

'Why?' I stuttered, but then I immediately regained control. 'Of course, but what do I say to them?'

I was imagining the actual people. I thought of ringing the bell or knocking and giving them a food stamp.

'You're right . . . That's going to be a problem.' Zora started thinking.

'They're suspicious of postmen, you see. They hide from official letters,' I explained. 'They lie about the addressees being unknown when they're drafted . . .'

'Right, right.' Nikolaj was nodding. 'They are rightly suspicious. They've been disowned, getting decrees and decisions all the time. The government just takes away, every new government – it's normal in these parts, ever since feudal times. The *kharaj*, the looting, the Balkans, and now suddenly . . . they get something. They'll think it's a trap and won't dare use the food stamps. They'll worry, be afraid. Those with weak hearts could have strokes. What times. What a country – you can't even do a good deed!'

We looked at each other in silence.

'But would you agree? Would you deliver the food stamps?'

44

'Of course. With pleasure.'

Nikolaj suddenly smiled widely.

'I've got an idea!'

He slapped the books and gave a loud laugh. His teeth glistened in the sun. 'What an idea!'

Zora gave him a surprised look and hugged him. I felt a little sting in my heart, I admit. 'That's what I like most about him, his ideas!' she said. 'These writers! They create something out of nothing!'

She kissed him on the cheek.

'What sort of idea?' I asked timidly.

'I have to think it through, work on it. Perhaps it's not the right one. See you tomorrow.'

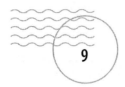

9

The next day I was prancing like a foal to get to their house as soon as possible. My knee was acting up, but I wasn't paying any attention to it. Faster, faster!

And nothing. The terrace empty, the door shut.

I wanted to ring the bell, but how could I? I didn't have a registered letter. Without mail, without an excuse?

Maybe it wasn't the right idea.

What did that even mean?

I'd heard a lot about the ideas of communism, of socialism, and I had a feeling his idea was really something that was created out of nothing, like Zora said. Not there before, and then it suddenly appears. A person is sitting and waiting – not even that, perhaps doing something else, something ordinary – and suddenly, an idea! I thought only great men had them: Marx, Engels, Stalin – well, not him; he wasn't supposed to be mentioned any more, though I thought of him every time I saw the pale stain on the wall – and Tito. Leaders of parties and countries. Could someone else also have an idea? Somebody I personally knew? I hadn't met anyone like that before. Nikolaj, whom I could almost touch?

Now . . . Do you know you can have thoughts and subthoughts at the same time? The first ones are slow cows

– they come, they lumber, they go – but the second ones, they're weasels. They whizz between cows' hoofs and usually get away before you get the chance to notice them. So, at the thought of her touching Nikolaj, a whole pack of subthoughts about Zora was unleashed. The line, the touching, her scent . . . I thought it better to hurry along my route.

I had trouble sleeping, because I was so interested in the idea. Suppose it wasn't the right one. How could you tell? The right one? Could I tell a right one from a wrong one?

Every morning I came around the bend left an image of the veranda in my memory. I was so tense and longed for signs of life so badly. Nothing. The second day, the third . . . The fourth day, when they were sitting there, drinking coffee, I would have walked right past them from sheer surprise. With my head switched off, my body would've just continued along the way; they had to wave at me to make me register them and sit down.

'We've been waiting for you,' Nikolaj said, and I was afraid he would reproach me for not ringing the bell. He went on:

'I think the idea was the right one.'

He looked to Zora, who gave him a big smile and squeezed his shoulder. She rocked forward and planted a kiss on his cheek.

He put away the books and laid his hands on the papers under them. Sheets, envelopes, food stamps.

'We're starting the German Lottery,' he said.

I was all eyes.

They were staring at me, and it didn't look as if they were going to explain anything.

After a while I noticed I was shifting in my seat, sighing, and I became embarrassed.

'But a lottery . . . It takes money away from people.'

'Not this one.' They shook their heads simultaneously.

'We're torturing him.' Zora nudged her husband.

'You're right, dear.' He turned to me: 'I'm sorry! I'll explain immediately. We can't just give the food stamps to those who need help. But we can tell them the country is organising a lottery and everyone gets a ticket. And then every ticket wins. Read it.'

He offered me a typed letter.

At the beginning it said the letter was being sent by Deutsche Lotterie, PF 1512, Berlin, Deutschland – I'll never forget that – and then it went on in Slovenian. I can't remember the exact words, but it said the government of the Federal Republic of Germany, which was aware of its responsibility for the war and regretted it deeply, was organising a lottery in which the citizens of all the countries that suffered under the Nazi occupation could participate. For each country, they had opened a department that would organise correspondence in the native language and provide suitable winnings. They could not pay damages to everyone, but they could give lottery tickets to those who had suffered the greatest injustices and needed help the most. A draw would be held once a week. They asked the chosen ones to keep the secret to themselves, because an envious crowd could drive the lottery to bankruptcy. The German government would finance the fund to the extent its resources would allow. They said they were sorry once again and thank you very much. The letter was also a ticket, and the number was . . .

There was an empty line and then, in the middle, a six-figure number was typed, underlined with dashes.

After another empty line, the letter said that the recipient should return the ticket if the person thought it had been sent to the wrong address or give it up for someone who needed help more and let the lottery know the person's details.

I didn't understand very well, though I read it three times.

After a while Nikolaj jumped in. 'Look. The idea seemed so good –'

His eyes met Zora's. They smiled, another sting in my heart.

'– that I prepared everything. The envelopes . . . I typed ten letters, had seals made . . .'

He placed the letter on the table and opened an ink pad. Then, picking it up by the handle, he dipped the seal and with a firm hand, without overdoing it, marked the bottom of the letter.

We stared at the mark.

Now, let me tell you why professions need uniforms and state seals and forms: because without them everything is just empty words. When you see a uniform and a seal, it's serious. The word becomes flesh. The idea becomes law.

The letter became real, official.

Nikolaj made a scrawl over the mark. Then he took the envelope and marked that too. The envelope also became real.

I only have my common sense to thank that I managed to express doubt despite the impressive display:

'But it doesn't exist?'

'It exists as far as we and our needy citizens are concerned. They'll get the food stamps next week.'

'But it doesn't really exist?'

'How come? The food stamps aren't food either. You can't eat them, but when you show them in the shop, they fill your stomach. It's the same with a lottery that lets you win every time.'

'Everyone?'

'Yes, everyone.'

I liked that. In those days, Yugoslavia already had a lottery, but a capitalist one, and only a chosen few won. But the German Lottery was a true, socialist lottery; everybody won the same.

'Why German?'

Nikolaj sighed and leaned back against his chair.

'A good question. I've given this much thought. If we said it was Slovenian, Yugoslav, then we'd be doing something the state is already doing. And the government cannot stand competition. It wouldn't be good. For us. German – that's understandable. They're guilty, so let them pay. Everyone will agree and accept our gifts without hesitation.'

'What if someone reports it?'

'That's another reason why it's better for the lottery to be German and not ours. We don't have diplomatic relations. They cannot ask officially. We must have some spies in Berlin, but I doubt they'd risk sending one to check on post office boxes. After all, it's mail from the imperialist West, from a country we've been at war with until recently. We might be on the brink of one again.'

'German stamps …'

'Ha! You don't miss a thing. Nothing gets past you. You're sharp, you!' he smiled broadly and added:

'I said seals, not *a* seal!'

He pulled out another seal from under the papers and dipped it in the ink pad.

'Get ready for this. The black market knows no limits.'

He opened a grey book, and there were rows upon rows of identical stamps with some sort of a lacy crown. He picked up one, looked at me above it, and spat at its back too loudly before sticking it on the envelope. He postmarked it with the other seal in one move.

I leaned forward. I could only read *Berlin* clearly; the date was smudged.

'It's carved that way,' Nikolaj said with pride.

We stared at a real Berlin letter.

The coffee had been drunk, the bag was pushing under my ribs, and the wind was turning up the corners of letters.

I was wondering what the national heroes would have done in my place. They sacrificed their lives for the good of the people. Perhaps I could help at least ten people without having to die.

'Yes,' I said. 'Yes.'

They smiled, relieved.

I followed their lead and we shook hands, many times.

Nikolaj asked me to make a list of the ten neediest people by the next day, which I dismissed with a wave of the hand. I'd made it the previous night. The old, suffering faces of the poor souls kept appearing before my eyes as I was thinking about good deeds and food stamps. I'd written down their names and addresses on a piece of paper. When Nikolaj picked it up, he stopped.

'One more thing. You also pick up mail from the mailboxes in the evening, don't you?'

'Yes.'

'The replies, if there are any, have to be picked out. You know that.'

'Of course.'

'If anyone goes to the post office and mails a reply from there, and then the answer comes back that the addressee is unknown . . .'

'I know.'

He smiled and ran to the house with the envelopes. I heard the typewriter, and I couldn't believe a man could type so quickly.

Zora and I were left alone.

I should have gone, I was running late with my delivery. I scratched my Code of Practice booklet, which had started to give me an itch in my breast pocket.

'I know,' she said. 'I know. There are matters of the heart. But please . . .'

She leaned forward.

Her scent – it escaped through her cardigan, which opened before me like a door.

'I'm only human, only a woman . . . I was so lonely . . . Please, understand and keep our secret.'

'Yes, yes,' I stuttered and watched her as she had to stand on tiptoe to get close to me.

She squeezed my shoulder and dropped a brief kiss on my cheek.

'Thank you.'

I don't remember what happened after that. I came to at the end of my delivery route, when there was nothing left in my bag but the ten letters being sent by the German Lottery.

Give my best to everyone at home. Bye.

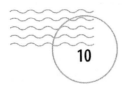

10

can't believe it, something to sign again. What municipal service tax? Just cancel. You're right; you think of everything. See? Like I've said, the government only takes away. I won't look for my glasses now. Show me with your finger. So many copies? I know, I know.

Where was I last time? Oh, yes . . .

I put the letters in my inside pocket and stood in front of the bathroom mirror, checking whether they showed.

I didn't think I was capable of hiding and smuggling. Maybe because in the mirror, left is actually right and the other way around? We see the inverted image of ourselves and say, that's what we look like! I was excited, though. I cut myself shaving, but I was shaving more out of wish than out of need anyway; there were only a few downy hairs growing on my chin.

At work, I had the feeling that Lovro and Janez knew everything, though the first one was shaking evenly and the second one took him out for a walk as usual. When the manager dragged his finger across the mail, I was all ears, checking if he could hear the sound of my sweat dropping between my buttocks. When the clock finally struck eight, I had to stop myself from running off on my rounds. I was breathing heavily as I crossed the bridge, my head was spinning, and I preferred not to look at the water. Water is like an abyss; sometimes it calls to you, when you're not right. Remember this and stay away from it at those times.

I was nervous delivering the first letter and looked left and right many times as I stood in front of the letterbox. Then I told myself, you're a postman, you're doing your job, who would know you took on a bit more? I felt better. It suited me that Zora and Nikolaj were not sitting on the veranda. I passed by quickly. I only noticed with the last letter how much effort Nikolaj had put into it. He creased the envelopes a little, not too much, just along the edges, traces of dust here and there, the hardness of the paper softened with fingers. The letters really looked as if they'd come from Berlin. I remembered the partisans who were shouting under the hospital windows 'To Berlin! To Berlin!' when the war was drawing to its end.

Berlin, Berlin, I kept repeating, and it sounded nice. Finally the time came for this terrible city to become human. Let our people associate it with food, not with bombs.

Marija was weeding the garden and Ivan was sitting on the bench, just raising his head. He winked at me and we both moved to the table; the chair was already waiting for me.

I turned down the drink. I had a feeling they'd sensed my excitement.

Berlin, Berlin, I repeated in my head and laid the letter down in the middle of the waxed tablecloth.

They leaned forward.

'It's addressed to both of us,' Marija said.

'Nothing to worry about.' I tried to calm them.

'From Germany?' Ivan added.

'But we don't know anyone there, do we?'

Ivan's bald head moved slowly over the letter.

'It's a lottery.'

'Has everybody received it?' Marija gazed at me hope-fully.

'I can't say, madam – comrade, I mean. An official secret. But it's nothing to worry about. That's all I can say.'

Ivan was already about to tear open the envelope, but he stopped. He pulled his hands away and the letter lay there between us. We were silent. I noticed their eyes didn't meet that time, not once. When I think about it now, it seems I disturbed their peace. But the only thing I knew then was I had to hurry along my delivery route as soon as possible, despite my knee giving me a hard time.

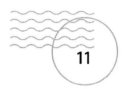

11

Three replies came back. I picked out the letters, hid them, and rang at Nikolaj and Zora's place the same evening. Nikolaj opened them with a special knife. He had to explain to me that it wasn't really sharp. The device was designed only for opening letters, which I thought was the height of luxury. In poverty, there isn't a single thing that serves only one purpose.

I felt a sting in my heart. We were opening other people's mail, which was against the rules. At the time I wasn't yet aware there was also something else that caused me pain. The first layer of my moral core had peeled away. I consoled myself that opening other people's mail might be a bad thing, but the addressee didn't exist, or rather, we were the addressee. I realised with surprise: we were the German Lottery! Suddenly, I looked proudly at the seal lying on the table. The letters had arrived at the right address.

One of the correspondents didn't want anything to do with the Germans, another advised us we could stick our ticket up Adolf's arse, while a lady comrade wrote a long explanation that Nikolaj read out loud. Her sons had died fighting the enemy for freedom and a better life. Her husband died in a concentration camp, and she had barely survived. Nikolaj really knew how to stress the right words when reading. At the end we were all sobbing with our heads bowed. He put the letter away and added:

'I respect her.'

None of the remaining seven wrote back to suggest anyone else instead. Nikolaj asked me to choose three new townspeople in need and put them on the list.

He typed their addresses on the envelopes and put in the initial letters.

'I couldn't wait,' he said. 'I've prepared everything for next week's draw today. It's the idea! It gives a man such power, such strength he could move mountains if they stood in the way. The greatest enemy of an idea is time. We cannot hasten it; we can only ignore it. Look, Toni, everything's here, everything for the next week.'

He showed me seven envelopes with the names of the winners. The German Lottery was sending all of the recipients the list with the winning numbers. Their numbers were among them, and the rewards were enclosed. If they wished to stay in the game, they had to write back. Nikolaj folded a letter and put it into an envelope. When he picked up the list, he opened it slowly for us while his eyes gleamed with pride. From top to bottom there were numbers, stacked into columns. I can still see them clearly, eight columns.

'Why have you gone to all this trouble?' Zora asked him.

'This is the best part for me. It's pure poetry, numbers, numbers. If you take a good look, you'll see it's meximeter.'

He said something like that and started explaining; I didn't understand very well. The numbers rhyming or repeating or something – writers' stuff.

'Perfectionist.' Zora squeezed his shoulder and kissed him on the cheek.

I felt a twinge. I won't talk about this any more but you can imagine – every time she touched him I felt a sting under my Code of Practice booklet.

The envelopes were open, waiting only for the coupons.

'Tell me, Toni, who is the poorest? Who suffers the most?'

'A comrade . . . lady from 14 Hero Zupan Street.'

I saw her before my eyes, the old lady, bent from all the suffering. She often stopped and when she looked at me tears started pouring down her cheeks. Sometimes she told me about her family and friends, who were only memories now. I sighed.

Nikolaj reached into his pocket and pulled out a banknote I'd never seen before. A nude woman with small breasts was holding a circle from which lines radiated. I looked to Zora, embarrassed, and immediately remembered her cleavage. I blushed, again, angry with myself. A naked woman. So what? It was only a drawing. In the middle was printed '5 fünf Deutschmark'. There was talk about building a different Germany, but I wasn't so sure they would succeed, since they were putting immoral pictures even on their money.

I watched Nikolaj in astonishment as he stuffed the banknote into the envelope for the weepy old lady, while he put food stamps in all the rest.

He sealed the envelopes and leaned back with the expression of a man who has done his job well.

'I like to share, when there is something to share,' he added after a while and started inspecting his glasses.

I knew what Zora would do, so I looked away.

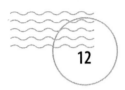

12

The winning letters gave me everything I was missing in my job: seven letters, seven pieces of good news. No dead, missing, jailed. No taxes, no drafts. I cannot describe the pleasure I felt while delivering them the next week. Especially to the weepy old lady! I imagined her gaping at the German banknote. How much would she get for it on the black market? Maybe she would even ask me if I could exchange it. I smiled to myself. Nikolaj was right when he talked about secrets. I had a wonderful feeling of kind-hearted superiority, without the ugliness. I had the knowledge; she didn't. An essential difference would soon appear between us. I was already her benefactor, carrying a gift for her, while she was still a slave to her troubles, not knowing what was coming.

Everything was back to normal at Marija and Ivan's. I put the letters in the middle of their table and their eyes met as usual, not bothered by my delivery. They included the letters in their peace. The moments I spent with them still felt like being gently covered by the branches of a weeping willow.

Luckily I retired before postmen started delivering only garbage. Is there anything else in letterboxes nowadays but raffles and prize draws? Actually, everyone just wants to *get* money. They give away very little of it. Now I have enough time, and I can see what happened in the past more clearly than what's happening now, I ask myself: were we ahead of the times with the German Lottery? The only difference was that we were idealists, and those were idealistic times. The communists wanted to hand out happiness to people in a big way. We wanted to do it in a small way, giving everyone as much as we could afford.

I know, soon everything went wrong – with both communism and the German Lottery – but the idea . . .

Oh, well. Maybe people aren't made to bring each other happiness.

In the evenings I picked out the answers with shimmering anticipation.

We paid out the winnings once a week. The day before, Zora and Nikolaj invited me for supper. We had dishes I'd never tasted before. Nothing like the stews they'd been making at the People's Kitchen. I'd better admit it, I became spoiled. After the Monday suppers, Tuesday lunches at the canteen didn't seem all that tasty.

An early summer arrived and the heat. I got a summer uniform, which made it harder to hide the letters, but I wasn't thinking that my colleagues and the manager could see through me, so they didn't. The weepy old lady couldn't hold out any longer. She moved away to her relatives. Before she went, she said goodbye, soaking the shirt on my chest while hugging me. I suggested a new name to be put on the list.

It all became a habit. The closed envelopes Nikolaj gave me, smuggling them to the post office, delivering them, picking out the answers in the evenings, delivering them to

Nikolaj. I asked him why he wanted the winners to write back, and he gave me his reasonable explanation:

'What if somebody didn't want our help? What if we were wasting it on someone who didn't really need it? And there's something else too: people are built to be active and cause results through their actions. If the tickets just kept coming, they'd be like the weather, beyond our control. Now, people have a feeling they've asked for the tickets, received them because of their own will, and earned their winnings through their actions. Have you ever read stories about Indians? Have you heard about the primitive tribes who dance for the rain and the sunshine?'

I hadn't, but I remembered the processions against droughts and floods.

'Well done.' He went on, 'You're a good observer. It's the same thing. I mentioned the natural elements earlier. When it comes to weather, we don't want to depend on someone else, even if it's God. We pretend we can influence him by praying, rituals. It's in our nature to force others to bow according to our will. That's why the German Lottery is only for those who want to play.'

The factory was opened by the leading Slovenian politicians. The comrades drove from Ljubljana, the capital of the republic, in the biggest black limousines I'd ever seen, and the announcer began:

'Now let us listen to the official speech of Mr Comrade Minister . . .'

It was good to see even educated people were having trouble switching between comrades and misters. I had a feeling the audience around me was snickering on the inside, though I couldn't be sure, because there were many policemen in the crowd, in uniforms and in plain clothes, so no one dared do anything but clap at the right moments.

Mr Comrade Minister dedicated most of his speech to spies that were everywhere among us. They'd just sentenced a group in Ljubljana that communicated in coded letters but didn't count on the alertness and intelligence of our agents. They'd broken the code and the group. I stopped listening at that point, because I remembered a neighbour from the hill opposite our homestead, who was shot by the Germans during the war. They thought she was informing the partisans by arranging the washing on the line. I found the world of codes completely mystifying and had great respect for those who could read them. A very special breed of people indeed.

The apartment block was filling up. They were raising two additional blocks. An engineer's family moved into the empty house that had belonged to the weepy old lady. I was glad she'd sold the property successfully and was able to raise money so she wouldn't be a burden to her relatives. The workers mostly moved here, to this side of the town, while the houses on the other side of the river were in high demand among the management of the factory. By summer, some of the home-owners, two lottery winners among them, sold their houses to the newcomers. There was never a shortage of lonely poor people, so I immediately added two new names to the list.

I wasn't only looking forward to the letters in which we delivered happiness. Every time I was about to enter the house, wind up the bell, my heart skipped a beat because I would see Zora. I knew she was married, and I respected Nikolaj – his wits, his literary ideas. I knew I couldn't compare to him. How could I come up with something so complicated, and useful at the same time, as the German Lottery? Sometimes Zora wouldn't even glance at me, but other times I would catch her staring at me with a strange look. I wanted to get her out of my mind, but during the nights when I struggled hardest not to think of her, I had to go to the bathroom more often.

She seemed out of reach. Beautiful and smart, married. I had nothing Nikolaj didn't have, but he had so much more, things I couldn't even imagine. Sometimes I was angry with myself for not taking the chance when he was in prison, but I quickly came up against my moral core, which was very near the surface where those things were concerned, and told myself: NO! Never! To take advantage of a woman in her moments of weakness – never!

During summer, my knee was worse than during winter. It was harder to walk, and I developed a bad limp halfway into my route. Lovro and Janez were moaning about the numbers of newcomers, so I took over the building where I lived. It didn't mean a lot of additional work, because the letterboxes in an apartment block are all in one place, and if the letters are sorted correctly, you just grab the bunch from your bag and, holding it in your left hand, take the letters one by one and push them through the slots.

No one is born with a postal brain. You have to develop one. When you begin to think like a postman – it took a couple of months in my case – there's nothing better than sorting mail. You see the streets in your head, you move between the houses – weightless, bodiless, no limping – you glide, you're everywhere at the same time. You skip a few houses, go back a couple of streets. You see everything. Faces, people – you know everything about everybody. You know their dogs and relatives. The newspapers they're getting, letters they're receiving and those they're sending. Postcards, official letters, everything. All of them are in your head. You carry all of them with you, thousands of them, and you're the link between them.

I'm not sorry I became a postman, and I never have been.

Even now, I sometimes close my eyes and go through my delivery route.

The route in 1950, in 1960, in 1970 – pick a year and I'll travel through it. The houses that are gone, the roads that have been dug up. There's supposed to be a thousand or three thousand – I don't know how many – people living here, but when you go over their faces, decade by decade, if you deliver their mail again, here, on this bed, when you see all of them at the same time, the same people young and old, over the period of forty years, all the events in their lives, the joys and the sorrows, you've got all that in your head. Not just thousands of people, but thousands multiplied by each event, by each period. So many faces of the same people in so many years, so many expressions, situations. You know most of them are dead now. They've left, like you will leave – you, who are the bond between what's past and what's to come – like everything will . . . There's a certain beauty in that – the way everything leaves, leaves, leaves.

Ah, you're leaving too?

I really got carried away, didn't I? Next time remind me where to pick up: one of the letters for the German Lottery was too thick.

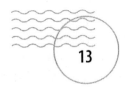

13

You don't need to remind me. The story of the German Lottery won't leave me. I must tell it!

So, one of the letters was too thick.

My hands were trained. I picked out the letters addressed to Berlin and started to hide them, when one of them stuck between my fingers. It was too thick. It got caught between my thumb and index finger, and I had to use force to fold it. By then I already had the postman's touch. I could tell it contained four or five sheets. I held it up to the light, and I could have sworn I saw some smaller shadows among the large sheets.

A terrible suspicion.

At home I boiled some water and unsealed the envelope. I had every right. The letter was addressed to me too.

There were five old, worn one-German-mark banknotes in the letter. The pensioner from 33 Hero Zemlji Street wrote that he had those old marks, which must still be accepted in Germany, at home, so he was sending them to buy the ticket.

Buy the ticket?!?!

I opened all the other letters.

In each of them there was a banknote, five German marks, the one with the nude woman.

People were ordering the tickets. One was even complaining because the German Lottery allowed you to buy only one ticket a week. Whoever was supplying the banknotes on the black market probably couldn't believe his luck.

Their faces flashed before my eyes. Marija and Ivan never complained, though it can't have been easy for them. And I was the unsuspecting pawn wheedling money out of them! And what about the rest? These poor people who had shared their grief, their misery with me were buying tickets for five German marks? Each week? Had they been lying? Was it possible that those who complained the most were not the ones who suffered the most?

I was enraged. For the first time in my life. At first I didn't even know what was the matter with me, I felt strange. I was looking for the right expression, and then I surprised myself: rage.

Zora and Nikolaj were lying to me. The townspeople were lying to me. Did they think I was so naïve?

It's a terrible feeling when you finally discover something that everybody else knows. You feel dirty, not whole, lacking.

I was winding up the doorbell with the force my brothers used on my ears.

Zora immediately knew something was wrong.

I entered without being invited in.

Nikolaj was sitting at the table, laid for dinner. There was a place for me too.

I threw the letters on the table. Some banknotes slipped out.

'You're selling the tickets!'

Zora turned to Nikolaj. She wanted to say something.

He raised his arms towards her as if he wanted to stop her and push her away at the same time.

'She doesn't know!'

Zora was looking from me to him, puzzled.

'What don't I know?' she said finally.

Nikolaj put his hands on his chest. 'The decision was mine. All mine.'

I felt like crying, but I didn't want them to see my tears. 'I thought we were doing good deeds!'

'But we are!'

'How? How, if we're selling?'

'Think, Toni. Think. Think about what we are like. If we get something for free, we don't appreciate it. First, there's the desire; then, the action to fulfil it; and in the end, we have to pay for it. It's the natural order of things. The German Lottery has reached the third stage. It has grown organically. It's a living thing, in a way; it needs to grow and change.'

I didn't listen to him. I collapsed into a chair and couldn't hold back any longer. I started sobbing. I was ashamed, but I couldn't stop myself. I cried like never before. Wailing, unstoppable sobs.

I felt Zora's arms around my shoulders. She held me tight and I cried even harder. I was afraid I wouldn't be able to stop and started fighting back the tears, the pressure in my chest.

'Breathe. Breathe, kid,' Zora whispered, and finally, snapping for air in shudders, I somehow stopped and sat there like a wretch.

Nikolaj wiped his brow and sighed.

'Toni, Toni, there was no need for that. Listen to me, my friend, please.'

He pointed with his hand:

'Look, there are ten winning letters waiting for you here for next week. They're sealed, ready. They were prepared before you came. Unseal them, please. Take a look inside.'

I didn't move.

'Toni, please.'

I reached out with my trembling hand but had to bring it back a few times to rub my eyes and focus my vision. I slowly opened the first envelope, the second one, down to the last one. Banknotes fell out of them.

'Count it, please,' he said.

Twenty marks, ten marks, someone won as many as fifty marks. Altogether there were 180 marks on the table.

'And how much did they send?' he asked softly.

'Fifty.'

'Even less. Those old ones are not accepted any more.'

We fell silent.

'I thought we were still handing out food stamps.'

'Rarely. People prefer money. Ever since the factory and the People's Kitchen opened, the standard of living has improved. It's not that hard these days. We are entering the second half of the twentieth century, and I think this will be the age of money.'

Zora gave me her handkerchief with her name stitched on it. I still keep it.

Nikolaj went on:

'Like I've told you, people want to be active. They want to pay in, take a risk, because when they win, they feel like they've beaten their destiny. I'm sorry for not telling you sooner. Somehow I thought it was logical. You have an idea, you get it, and you think everyone else gets it too, which of course isn't the case. I'm sorry. Will you forgive me?'

I nodded.

'And another thing, look . . .'

He picked up a dark blue notebook and opened it.

'I keep a record for every winner. I put down how much money they pay in and how much they win. I'll tell you everything now, so there won't be any problems later on. Not everyone wins in the German Lottery, every time, now. If you're lucky every week, it's not luck any more, it's a habit. But I make sure everyone wins at least three times as much as they pay in. There is no lottery like ours. And there won't be one, because we're doing it for the greater good.

'Oh, and another thing: now they write the numbers they put their money on. You must have noticed that.'

Zora, who stood by my side, caressed my shoulder and kissed me on the cheek. I became flustered because her lips touched my wet cheeks, but she didn't seem to mind.

'I want to show something to Toni.' She turned toward the door leading to the hall.

Nikolaj frowned. 'Are you sure?'

'Yes. I think it's time.'

It seemed Nikolaj didn't entirely agree. He hesitated, but then he nodded.

Zora held me by the arm and helped me up. I was taller than her by a head, so I gently put away her arm and followed her.

We entered a long hallway and she took me to the first room. When she turned on the light, I couldn't believe my eyes. I thought I was standing in the middle of a castle, or at least that's how I imagined them in fairy tales. Antique furniture, paintings in golden frames, a beautiful radio, big as a wardrobe.

She was looking at me and waiting.

'I don't understand.'

'Nikolaj is wealthy, at least for these circumstances. Writers have always done well, and he's also from an old family. In socialism we're all equal, so we have to pretend we're poor. The house is shabby on the outside on purpose, the guest room's badly furnished. If somebody knew our secret, the state would confiscate everything. Nikolaj would agree to it, if everything went to the poor, but these antiques would end up in politicians' manors. You've been to the opening of the factory. You've seen their cars.'

I had, and what I'd seen triggered some subthoughts, but I didn't dare chase them, because there were so many policemen around. I knew what Zora was trying to tell me.

'Please, if you can, let him keep up his charity. He's a special type of person; there aren't many of his kind around. Let him share the crumbs of his property through the German Lottery. You saw yourself that people are better off, and we get by all right.'

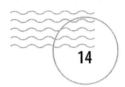

14

I'm proud that I was able to apologise to Nikolaj for the injustice I'd done him in real life because of something that was a figment of my imagination. I saw all sorts of things in my delivery rounds, but apologies were few and far apart. Obviously, distinguishing your problems from other people's problems is one of the hardest things in the world, because we don't notice where our actions end and the reactions of others begin.

After dinner we sealed the letters with the winnings, and I took them with me.

What was I saying? Oh, yes, about other people.

First, our parents build us, then our peers, and later our jobs; we are works in progress. What I wanted to say was that if we are created by average people, we turn out average too. Only now do I understand that I started thinking in a different way after that evening with Zora and Nikolaj. I stopped idolising the socialist equality of all people – not financial equality, but the idea that we all think and act the same. Because I met a man who could act differently, in a good sense. A righteous man, my mother's words came back to me. He has money and he gives it away – not boasting, not showing off. He's organised a complex system. The townspeople join, take a chance. Sometimes they win, sometimes they don't. And the good organiser sees to it that they always profit.

That night I dreamed about God, but I don't remember what.

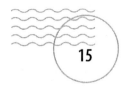

15

The next week, I received the first letter in my life. After sorting it correctly, I realised it was for me. I wanted to open it, but then I remembered the rules – postmen mustn't open letters. I held back, then had a thought that it was for me, a civilian, not a postal employee, so it became clear to me that I had to deliver it as a postman and take it from the letterbox as a private individual after work. I know, your generation thinks rules are naïve, don't you? You're young. You'll see. Stories about growing up are always stories about losing naïveté and conforming to rules.

Where was I?

Well, I delivered the letter, ran all the way along my route as hard as I could and opened it before I took off my uniform. I couldn't wait any longer.

It was a nice letter. I still keep it. Typed, elegant. It said Zora and Nikolaj were inviting me to a dinner, which would be held on Monday at 8 p.m. at 12 Hero Stane Street to celebrate the three months of the German Lottery. I should come dressed casually, which I didn't quite understand, because I only had one suit besides my uniform, and my hosts knew that. A really nice letter, official, stately even. The government was sending letters full of acronyms back then, like SKOJ, standing for the league of Yugoslav socialist youth; AVNOJ, short for the anti-fascist council of national liberation of Yugoslavia; and AFŽ, the anti-fascist women's front. That's how it was back then. Following the Russian model, I heard. The Russians have long titles they shorten, and we copied them, though our words are shorter than their contractions. What I wanted to say is that in the bottom of the letter it said RSVP, and for the next couple of days I kept wondering what sort of a Redistributing State Valorisation Panel it stood for.

They served dinner in the writerly, rich part of the house, at a long table, but unfortunately right in the middle of one of the numerous power cuts, so they had to bring in candleholders and we ate in candlelight. Nikolaj put on a black tailcoat that suited him, while Zora wore a dark violet dress that seemed as if it were alive. It glided and slithered over her, wrapped itself around her body, and fell downwards, over the chair, towards the floor. It shivered with her. I had to stop myself from reaching out and feeling the fabric that seemed magical, as if it were going to slip away and leave Zora . . .

I bit my lip, hard.

I said I didn't want wine, that I couldn't stand the sour taste, but they were insisting, saying it was sweet. And indeed, it tasted different from the wine my father and brothers used to drink. Its taste went to my stomach and its influence to my head. It drew my lips into an endless smile.

We had strange dishes. Zora told us what they were called, but they seemed harder to pronounce than to digest. I knew some of the ingredients, but most were new to me. The meal was good, no doubt, but I've always been one of those skinny guys who eat a lot, so at the end of the evening I secretly craved boiled potatoes and a sausage.

After the meal, she brought two coffees and tea for me. It had a peculiar, bitter taste. I had to put a lot of sugar in it, and she even wanted to pour milk into it, but I didn't let her. Nikolaj lit up and focused on each puff. He created it with inhalation, held it inside him, and then released it into the world, following it with his eyes until it dispersed.

'Toni . . .' he began, but instead of going on he said my name a few times, as if it were one of the smoke puffs he needed to follow until they died away.

'Toni, the German Lottery is celebrating three months of activities. We've made a lot of people happy. Thank you.'

He lowered his eyes. They both had wide smiles on their faces, and Zora reached out her hand for a moment and quickly touched the back of my hand.

I was angry with myself for always reacting the same way: blushing. Only this time I felt like crying. I didn't know why. I wasn't being reproached, but praised. I felt the same way, though. People truly are strange.

Zora was slowly dissolving sugar in her coffee. Nikolaj took off his glasses again, had a good look at them, and wiped away a speck with the tip of his napkin.

'Toni, ten people in this town are more content, happier I'd say, than three months ago. From the point of view of our century, it's nothing. Seventy million died in a single war, a war with serial number 2, which means the plan is to continue. But there are only three of us. And we've made ten people happy. So, Toni, here's to our three months. Cheers!'

He raised his glass and we clinked.

'Toni, you are country-born. You must have noticed every organism has its own course. It starts out little and helpless when it's born, it grows, matures, then stays unchanged for a time, and in the end it starts to wither and die. It's the same with societies, systems, countries, empires. The same. So, Toni, where in its cycle would you say the German Lottery was?'

My head was spinning, I began to blink and was barely able to focus my eyes.

I didn't know the answer.

I tried to guess it from his face, but all I saw was kindness.

I remembered the questions my brothers used to ask me. I tried to guess the right answer, but I always became confused and got a thrashing. But I wouldn't get thrashed now, even if I didn't give the right answer. I wished my father had been like Nikolaj, God rest his soul.

'How old is it?' Nikolaj asked softly.

'Three months.'

'Well?'

'It's young.'

'That's right, Toni. Bravo. Your answer is correct. The German Lottery is young. It's barely been born. Now, let's go back to nature. Let's take a kitten or a lamb –'

'A kid –'

'Right, Toni, a kid. Imagine it's encased, wrapped like a mummy . . .'

He noticed I wasn't following him.

'Imagine it's put in such a small room that it cannot grow any more. What will happen to it?'

'Errr . . . It will stay little?'

He shook his head.

'It'll die.'

Silence. I tightened the grip on my glass; my thumb slid and squeaked. It made an awful sound.

'Toni, every organism has to grow. Either grow or die. So' – he put out his cigarette and leaned down to my face – 'we're expanding the German Lottery to one hundred participants!'

Cutlery rattled and a chair scraped against the floor. Zora turned sharply towards her husband.

'Twenty!'

He slapped his hand on the table:

'A hundred!'

She gave me a quick, secret glance and then focused on Nikolaj again.

'Twenty!'

I could never have imagined she could go from being relaxed one minute to being furious the next. She was fuming, and I could hear the air hissing through her nostrils.

Nikolaj shook his head.

'Wife, don't you forget about our agreement. Who's the boss here?'

He rapped on the table with his outstretched fingers.

Anger gave her an altogether different beauty. The former was graceful and gentle, helpless, but the latter was sharp and focused. I thought Nikolaj would burst into flames under her gaze.

'Don't be foolish. It's too much. Even twenty is risky.'

'A hundred, and that's my final word.'

Nikolaj turned to me and smiled. My eyes slipped to Zora, who was gripping a napkin in her hands, wringing the dry fabric. She shot up and marched through the door, not running, but pounding her heels into the floor like St George.

Nikolaj cleaned his glasses until the house became completely quiet.

'Women,' he murmured.

'Maybe it really is too much.' I asked, 'Who will pay for all of it?'

He flailed his arms in the air.

'Writers are doing well, don't you worry. My new novel will be published next year.'

He lit a new cigarette. 'You want one?'

I said no.

'Toni, if you're making ten people happy, and you could make a hundred people happy, then why go only for twenty?'

I didn't have an answer. 'But Zora –'

'Zora is a woman,' he cut in. 'Their curse is in the numbers. Look, we men went to the battlefields. We're used to multitudes, to thousands, millions! I admit, our natures mostly send us to our graves, but we're used to wars that involve larger and larger masses. Masses are our natural habitat. We can either engage in mass destruction or take care of the masses.

'Women on the other hand . . . How many children can a woman have? Twenty. Right? A number you've heard earlier tonight. Or ten. These are the numbers a woman can take care of. She can imagine them, because she can compare them to the circle of her influence, her family. Zora would increase the family of the German Lottery winners only up to twenty. Everything else is beyond her imagination. I'm sorry. You got caught in a battle of the sexes, completely unawares. Because, I admit, before dinner, even I thought twenty was the right number. But I did some calculations during dinner – I must have seemed preoccupied – and I realised the right number was one hundred.

'If you agree, of course. There is no German Lottery without you. You're the field man. You're what makes it tick, the delivery man. You're the legs of the German Lottery, its basis!'

I thought he might be drunk, the way he flailed his arms, looking at the ceiling.

He noticed my silence and my gaze, stopped, and bowed his head.

'I'm sorry. I got carried away. Wine and winning an argument with a woman can get the better of even the firmest of men.'

He poured the rest of the wine into our glasses. We clinked.

'You agree?'

'What about Zora?'

'I'll persuade her. Don't worry. Female nature is like a river, it goes around the obstacles, while men are like rocks.'

'If Zora agrees . . .'

'Yes, yes,' he waved as if my words were flies. He started inspecting his glasses for specks of dust again. The drink suddenly went to his head.

'This is strange . . . These glasses. You can't really see them, because you wear them right before your eyes. All the time specks get stuck to them, like blind spots. If you didn't remove them, soon you wouldn't see anything any

more. Would you even notice your sight was slowly growing worse? You could make out less and less of the world,
and you'd think it's the way it's supposed to look. Cleaning
the glasses is a never-ending struggle for reality.'

He said the last sentence with his brow on the table. I
sat and waited. There wasn't a sound in the house. Wind
howled from behind the shutters, the candles were burning
down. I went to the light switch and turned it on. Luckily
the power cut was over, so I blew out the candles and left.

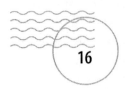

16

The next day, when I walked past the shop at the beginning of my route, I met Zora, who was just coming out the door. I had to look twice before I recognised her without those little dresses of hers. She wore a long skirt and a brown cardigan to town, covered her head with a scarf, and held a straw shopping bag under her arm. I thought she wanted to blend in with the old comrades who went shopping at that time of the day.

We walked a part of the way together.

'I'm worried,' she began. 'I'm worried about Nikolaj. He's a good man, maybe even too good for this world.'

'He said you could manage financially –'

'Yes, we can, for now. But a hundred people . . . I'll be frank with you, as always. Perhaps the government won't find out about ten people who are playing the imperialist lottery, but a hundred? They'll find us out, sooner or later. That won't be good. I've already lost him once . . . You remember, don't you?'

I blushed again.

'A woman in these parts and in these times needs a man. I'm worried. Slovenians are a small nation. Everything needs to be small. We're created for invisibility, our masters mustn't notice us. The authorities are above us, far away.

On the surface we're submissive, but in secret we do things our way. And Nikolaj – it went to his head. He's reading *The Will to Power,* that sort of thing. He's losing his Slovenian caution and smallness. I'm worried.'

'What if you tried talking to him?'

I limped more than was necessary.

'Do you agree with him? Tell me. I appreciate the truth.'

'Yes.' How hard it was for me to say it! 'If he can help a hundred people, why not? The idea of the German Lottery is beautiful.'

'You really think so?'

I nodded. 'I thought about it a lot. How can someone have such an idea out of nothing? I'm a part of something we're creating together for the first time! Out of nothing!'

She smiled. 'I'm glad. I see you've been captured by the idea too. It must be good, really. Tell me honestly, would you change it?'

'What do you mean?'

'Would you expand it from ten to a hundred?'

I felt trapped.

'Errr . . .'

'You wouldn't, would you? If Nikolaj hadn't suggested it. A man – there always has to be a man pushing an idea forward. It's the way of the world. The rule of men – he, a hero, and the masses following him. We've seen where it ends. Why not work quietly, on a small scale?'

I had a feeling again that her heels were pounding harder into the pavement.

'Look, I like the idea too, but it mustn't get out of hand. A hundred is too many.'

'Maybe it's not.'

'We'll have to move again,' she said, and I didn't understand.

'Excuse me?'

'Oh, nothing, nothing. Tell me about ideas. Haven't you got them?'

I shook my head. I was ashamed.

She briefly put her hand on my shoulder, but she didn't kiss me on the cheek.

'Don't worry about it, Toni, really. Most people haven't got them. Where would we be if everyone had them? Only a few individuals have ideas, and other people carry them out. That's the way of the world. The problem is that those who are meant to carry out the ideas are captured by them and adopt them. They forget their place. Marx had an idea, right? And Stalin is carrying it out as his own, and not very well, as we hear.'

She stopped, and I did the same, though I otherwise always followed the rules in public. She was speaking in a strange, absorbed way:

'The secret to the success of a man who has good ideas is in finding people who don't get captured by them and snatched away. That's all.'

I'd never seen her so deep in thought before. Her brow was alive with little wrinkles.

She didn't say anything else as we walked to the end of the bridge.

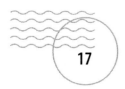

17

Expanding the German Lottery caused quite a few problems for me. It's not easy to smuggle a hundred letters to the post office, especially in the summer, under a thin shirt. In the end, I divided them into several days, which also made collecting the replies easier. Once I . . . No, that wasn't then. I can't remember! Even now that whole month is one big mess – workers and engineers coming, delivery routes that had been the same for a century changing suddenly, new names and surnames. One moving away, another one moving in. No wonder old people were leaving the town. A wave of industry, life and noise smashed through it suddenly and decisively. When the factory started running, we all slept badly for a few days and talked louder, before we got used to it. We're like magpies; we only see and hear the things that are new. As soon as we get used to them, they sink into the background and cease to exist.

My partners in the German Lottery were excited too. Nikolaj spent his days typing the letters, one cigarette burning in the ashtray while he sucked on another one. The margins of his sweat stains grew under his armpits. Zora was always frowning, thinking and thinking. She seemed alert, like a calf the moment my brothers started moving around it, getting everything ready, the butcher starting to sharpen the knife. She begged me a few more times to talk to Nikolaj, which I did, but he wouldn't listen to me. It was no use. It's true that my words sounded empty even to me. The thing grabbed me too. The lottery was expanding. I thought people were in a better mood while the world was being changed. It probably wasn't just because of us. Summer was here, and the factory offered an abundance of jobs.

If I think about it now . . . It was a time of decisions, and we all had to face them. They put up a bar next to the shop. Lovro and Janez didn't need to take a walk across the bridge now, and they saved too. I heard them praising their choice: no sitting down, waiting for the waiter; you came, stood, drank, paid less, and left. On your feet the whole time, a modern man in modern, hurried times, always ready to move on to the next successful venture.

I've wandered. I think it's because my legs can't carry me any longer and my head follows any thought that has to do with walking. Well, Nikolaj was getting more and more absorbed and self-sufficient. He didn't even talk much. Zora was concerned for his health. It seemed she loved him deeply. I had to admit that, despite the stinging under my CP booklet. Once she even spoke to me about love. She asked me:

'Do you know what love is?'

I didn't know the answer, but I didn't want to stay quiet, so I stuttered that love is when two people get married.

'Do you remember seeing love in your childhood?' she went on, as if I hadn't answered her.

I racked my brain even more.

'No.' I shook my head.

'What did you see?'

'My mother needed my father to keep up the farm. My father needed my mother to cook and take care of the animals. And my brothers, they slowly took over part of the work.'

'Yes, that's it. You're right,' she agreed. 'They needed each other. But did they love each other?'

I recalled their faces, my mother's and my father's, with ease, but I'd already begun to forget my brothers by then. I don't want to remember them now at all. What did they ever do for me, except thrash me? You know, kid, the main pleasure of outliving everybody is in the fact that everybody thinks 'he'll remember us', and you – you just say 'up yours' and forget them.

Ha, ha! You think it's strange I got upset? It's true, the thrashings were seventy years ago, five countries ago, and God knows how many leaders ago, but in some cases time passes more slowly in our minds, or not at all.

What was I saying?

Oh yes, I couldn't say they loved each other.

But I refrained from repeating what Nikolaj had told me once: love and the struggle for survival don't go hand in hand.

'They sure did need each other though,' I agreed.

We were standing on the veranda. The washing was flapping again, almost dry, even though I'd been delivering mail only a couple of hours by then. It was the beginning of the hot summer and my knee was cracking worse than ever.

'Look,' her eyes went over the rooftops that were visible through the trees, 'you're a postman, you see people, you know everything. Do they live together because they love each other?'

'There are these two pensioners . . .'

'One single couple? And what about everybody else?'

I thought about it a lot, even afterwards, and I couldn't give a different answer than I did back then:

'I don't think so.'

'Love is overrated. More people find pleasure in work than in love,' she said, and she asked me if I would like a coffee.

It was a very telling sign about how absorbed she was. Otherwise, she knew very well I didn't drink it.

'I'm worried about him too,' she glanced towards the door. The noise of key-punching was coming in bursts. He was typing addresses on the envelopes. 'The idea has started to consume him. It's stronger than him. He's just a slave now, but he isn't aware of it. He can't sleep. He lies by my side, and I can hear him murmuring women's names. Toni, I know what you men are like – when you try to put yourselves to sleep by counting your exes, you're really at the end of your tether.'

Fear is contagious. It stayed away from me for a long time, but once it got hold of me, it didn't let go. Not right then, after the talk with Zora. Something else had to happen first.

The German Lottery paid out the jackpot.

Yes, of course, next time. Goodbye!

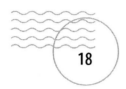

18

It was in the middle of July, the town was getting busier and busier with the comings and goings, people were moving houses, I could hardly keep up with all the changes, when –

I need to sign? TV cancellation? It's true, I don't use the one at home any more. I have no use for it with my eyesight.

Hold on, hold on. Six sheets? Where are my glasses?

I can't find them now. Where do I sign? Here, here . . . So much paper. They're crazy! You need my identity card and money for notarisation too? Again? Where is this country going? Piles and piles of forms for nothing! Every time they make a new country, in every revolution, they promise the next one will be economical, but it keeps getting worse and worse.

All right, that's settled.

Drat. What was I saying?

The newspaper headlines were full of the Korean War, and it suddenly looked like World War III was about to start there and not here. It sounds silly, but I was a little, just a little, disappointed.

Well . . .

In the evening, I came for the letters, just like every

Monday. The room was getting more and more untidy, papers were lying around everywhere, and Nikolaj, who used to smell of aftershave and brilliantine, was starting to smell a little of sweat. He wasn't typing. He held the straw bag Zora used for shopping in his hands and gave it to me.

I was all eyes. 'Why so many?'

'Two hundred!' he said, and Zora staggered and leaned against the wall.

'The German Lottery is entering a new stage. Two hundred winners! Two hundred people headed for prosperity, for a better future!'

Now that I see him in my mind's eye, I believe his eyes shone brighter than the rims of his glasses for the first time. He stood before me, sweaty and hot, steaming. Was he sick? I turned to Zora for help.

If she swayed at the news before, she was standing firmly now, leaning forward a little, and I saw her eyes were calm. It sounds silly, but I got the feeling she'd made a decision and was at ease. She somehow didn't fit into that chaotic scene.

'OK,' she nodded. Slowly she picked up the empty cups from the table, put them on a tray, and left.

I tried explaining to Nikolaj that it was impossible for me to smuggle two hundred letters to work, even if I divided them into several days. I would have the same problem with the replies. I talked and talked and knew all along he wasn't listening to me. His answers were about something else. I can't remember what. We talked without listening; it seemed more and more hopeless. I felt as lonely as if I'd been sitting under the weeping willow. The water flows,

I talk, our languages have nothing in common, they can never meet.

You're leaving? You're in a hurry today, eh? Oh, you've found my glasses! I really must be senile. I'd never think of finding them there.

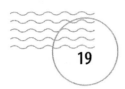

19

That evening, fear got hold of me. Lying in my bed, I watched the street lamps on my ceiling, a few shadows that moved by. In socialism, everything except the factories closed at 6 p.m., and there were no televisions, so ten in the evening was already considered late. I put the straw bag with two hundred letters behind the door. I couldn't see it, but I felt it like a thorn in my side.

Something strange was going on with Nikolaj. It made me think of the evil spirits my mother used to talk about. Was it possible they were still around, even in the times of scientific materialism? The man I had seen that evening did not have a lot in common with the man from a few months before. Calmness, erudition, learning – everything had disappeared from the surface like dust in a rain shower. If such a man could completely change in such a short time, could something similar happen to me? I tried to feel my legs, my arms, and my back on the bed . . . Was I still the same? Would something come along and change me? Would I no longer be myself? Would I do things I didn't want to do? Would an unknown power put me on like a glove and toss me away once it was done with me?

I felt lonelier than ever. No willow, no stones slowly breaking the surface of the water the way I wanted them to.

I wasn't really afraid of the authorities. Years later, we'd hear all sorts of things about jails and camps, murders, you name it, but when you're young you're the measure of things around you. And since I didn't see any bad intentions in myself, I didn't notice any in the world around me either.

I kept saying to myself I had a job to do, a straw bag full of letters to smuggle, so I had to be calm and rested the next day. But the more I tried to convince myself, the less sleepy I was.

My thoughts kept turning to Nikolaj. He counted his exes to fall asleep? Since I was still a virgin, there wasn't a lot to count. I cheated and started whispering:

'Zora . . . Zora . . . Zora . . .'

Every time I imagined her before me, summoned her from my memory, the images went further and further into the past, to the washing, the line, my lifted arms, her scent, the droplets of sweat that climbed up the rise before they went trickling into the valley . . .

Somebody was knocking very lightly.

Did I really fall asleep?

I jumped to my feet. It was still dark. Was I dreaming?

Knock-knock-knock.

I was shaking with fear. Was it morning already? Had the comrades in long leather coats come for me?

Was someone whispering my name?

Through a lock?

I opened the door to Zora.

She slipped by me, slid my hand off the door handle, and closed the door behind her.

'Shhh!'

Her scent, the rustling and shivering of her summer dress. Did I feel her hand on my shoulder, her hair that swept over my bare chest? The rooms were hot and stuffy, so I slept only in my pajama bottoms.

Was I even awake?

'Shhh!'

I nodded, so she stopped shushing me. She put her hands on my shoulders and pressed me down, her breath on my ear. She had been drinking coffee.

'I'm sorry. Did I wake you up? I want you to look at something.'

'What?'

'Find the letter for Marija and Ivan . . .'

She told me the full address.

'Why them?' I cried out with fear.

'You'll see.'

I took her back to the door and felt for the handle of the straw bag.

'Light?'

'No,' she gestured with her hand.

We both looked to the window. It wasn't built very carefully, so there was a lot of light spilling into the room despite the blinds being pulled down.

'On the other hand . . . You go to the toilet sometimes during the night, don't you?'

I remembered my dreams and said I did, glad my blushing was invisible in the dark.

'And you turn on the light?'

'Yes.'

'OK, turn it on then.'

I did as she said.

For a moment I thought it was really all a dream. I couldn't see her anywhere. Then I saw her, huddled in the corner, squatting, her back to the wall. She pointed to the straw bag.

I started going through the envelopes. It took me a while before I found the right one.

'Open it,' she mouthed.

I turned towards the cooker, but she prodded me and offered me an envelope she took from her purse. The same address was typed on it. I carefully tore the old envelope and started reading the letter.

It looked quite real.

But –

It said the person reading it was the lucky winner of the jackpot of the German Lottery:

1,000,000.00 D-mark.

I had to count the zeros, think about the commas and the decimal point, say it a couple of times in my mind before I could open my mouth:

'A mill –'

'Shush!'

'– ion?'

'Yes.'

'Even writers can't earn that much, can they?'

'No, they can't'

'How are you going to pay?'

She shook her head powerlessly. Her eyes were becoming larger and larger, and tears started trickling down her cheeks. She drew me to herself and buried her face into my skin. I felt each drop coming from her eyes on my chest. I'm ten times more hairy today than I was back then, when I was without a single hair. I really felt everything. Her lips, quivering with sobs; her bra, pushing into my stomach, rubbing and trembling when she breathed in; her hands, clinging to my neck; her hair, loosened, fragrant, lying on my shoulders. She moved away a bit, and the air in the room, which had seemed stuffy before, was now icy cold compared to her breath. She tried to wipe away her tears, stop crying, but she couldn't. She buried her face into me again. I put my arms around her and held her tight.

I'd have to think about the Practice Code . . .

I'd have to think about the Practice Code . . .

But I couldn't! She had covered too much of my skin, taken over too many of my senses. I could only welcome her in, my head completely empty. Not a thought inside me! Just the palms, the body, everything turning to her, trying to get covered by her, feel as much of her as possible, as deeply as possible, as long as possible. My nostrils breathed in her scent hungrily, my lips tasted her salty tears. I shut my eyes, because vision bothered me; there was too much of everything coming through other senses. I didn't want to look, I wanted to melt with her, inside her.

She was completely powerless. Slipping down, she couldn't cry any longer; there were only sobs, quiet. In spite of everything, she made a heroic effort not to be loud, not to be heard by the neighbours; female visitors were strictly forbidden. I fell back. I couldn't stay on my knees. I felt her above me, her scent, her tears. My head was spinning . . .

'Aah!' she said, appalled, and quickly moved away.

'What's the matter?'

She was looking in front of me. I followed her gaze. You

could see it through the light pajamas, of course you could see it.

It stood between us. I tried to push it down with my hands, but it didn't work. I scrambled backwards behind the bed and hid myself.

In a quiet and disappointed voice she said:

'I thought you were different. I thought you were special. I came here for help, and you're thinking only about one thing.'

She got up, straightened her dress, switched off the light, and left.

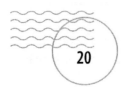

20

All right, you've come of age – not long ago, but still, we can talk like men.

Yes, I know.

I couldn't go back to sleep that night. I read the letter about the jackpot over and over. I knew it by heart, but I couldn't understand it. A million D-marks! I couldn't even work out how big a pile of banknotes with the naked woman that would make!

Naked women again! They lay waiting for me in my every thought. Yes, that's how I spent that night.

I didn't even dare to think about Zora and how I'd let her down. But it wasn't me! I would never . . . My subthoughts raced through my mind, screaming 'you would!'

It's true! It's true!

And so my thoughts moved in a circle: a million marks, naked women, a million . . .

When my alarm clock went off, I put the letter with the jackpot into the new envelope that Zora had brought, took some letters from the straw bag, and smuggled them to my delivery round.

People don't appreciate alarm clocks enough. It rang amid that mess, after the sleepless, feverish night, and how happy it made me! The alarm clock brings order. When it goes off, you don't think, guess, or decide. You already know when you're setting it what you'll have to do when it goes off. You'll have to wake up, get up, wash, dress, and go to work. Or on a trip. It doesn't matter. This is what matters: the alarm clock gives meaning to your actions and your thoughts. Not for a long time, that's true – maybe for eight or ten hours – but you use it every day. All your life. The alarm clock has given men more meaning than all the saints, prophets, philosophers and writers combined.

I still have it. It was this one. It doesn't work now, but I don't need it anyway. Even if it rang, I can't get up, I can't go anywhere. It's pointless.

How we paid out the jackpot?

Hang on, hang on. You've become interested? I had a feeling you were listening to me out of pity.

Ha, you little rascal. Tell me, how are you doing in school? You're studying economics, right? I think it's the right science for these times, the science of greed! What do you mean? Greed isn't mentioned in a single textbook, and you haven't heard it mentioned at lectures either? You're dealing with greed but you can't mention it, is that right? Are you sure this isn't a false science? Like having a postal university, where you calculate the amount of mail, but mustn't mention or even think about the senders and the addressees!

Let's leave this. Tell me how your parents are doing, and I'll go on with my story next time.

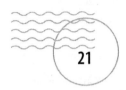

21

More than the thought about the million we would need to pay out, I was tortured by the feeling of guilt towards Zora. She came to me, the poor thing, in trouble, expecting my help, and I offered her only . . .

Bloody subthoughts, go away!

Zora's and Nikolaj's house didn't show any signs of life. Maybe Nikolaj had finally seen reason, realised he'd slipped up, and they'd both run away. The thought that I'd never see Zora again tore my heart.

I rushed past the houses, my thoughts everywhere and nowhere at the same time.

It was the first time I didn't sit down at Marija and Ivan's. I stuttered something about all the mail I still had to deliver and about being in a hurry. I wanted to put the letter calmly before them, but when I saw how my hands were shaking, I jerked my hand forward and crumpled the letter against the table. I blushed, said goodbye, and rushed off.

I continued along my delivery route, thinking: a million! How would Marija and Ivan take the news? What is Nikolaj really up to?

On my way back, I met Zora coming from the shop.

'Comrade postman, have you got anything for me?' she

asked very loudly. I rummaged around the empty bag until she came up to me.

'I'm sorry!' I said.

'It's all right. You're a man, you can't help it.'

I gave her a miserable look.

'Have you delivered the letter?'

'I have. Don't go home! How are you going to pay out a million? Has Nikolaj hidden himself?'

'Why would he hide?'

'Well, the winners are going to come and claim the million! It says in the letter they have to claim it personally.'

She looked at me as though she were searching for something. Finally she nodded, and there was a trace of a smile on her lips.

'I see,' she said. 'One of these nights, probably the day after tomorrow, we have to meet. I have to show you something. You've got to see with your own eyes. We'll meet behind the bunker. You know which one I mean? I'll let you know when.'

I nodded.

'Come decently dressed,' she added and turned away.

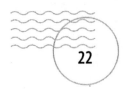

22

When I got the letter on Friday I was so tired, the thought of the Practice Code booklet didn't even cross my mind. It said I should be there at 10 p.m., only that, no signature.

I arrived a quarter of an hour early, but she was already waiting. I didn't see her at first, but then she appeared from the bushes. I jumped with fear. She constantly had to calm me down.

She wouldn't answer my questions. I would see for myself.

We went uphill, along a path that was almost completely overgrown in some places, and some parts were steep even for goats.

I tried to talk her into telling me what it was about. Fear was getting the better of me. We entered the border zone where the guards would shoot without warning. She didn't answer, so I just went along quietly, letting her lead me.

We stopped often, listening for the patrols. I was afraid there were land mines in the forest, but I didn't dare say anything.

There had been a full moon a couple of days earlier, and now and again a cloud swam across it, stretched out like a cigar. Once my eyes got used to the dark, I could see well, at least on the path, but between the trees it quickly became pitch black. I didn't know how long we'd been walking. Sometimes we saw the town through the branches, its lights more and more distant.

A thick larch rose before us, and Zora climbed up to it and hid behind it. She gestured at me to come closer. I breathed in her scent again, felt her next to me, but I could control myself. The fear of the guards, the freshness of the night, and besides, we were touching at the hips, so I wasn't afraid she would feel me. She had put on a pullover, so I could only sense her body under the wool. We were standing at the edge of the forest. There was a hollow underneath our feet that spread between the trees and sank into the darkness again. The silvery moonlight fell on the leaves. We waited and waited. I didn't dare speak. I only watched, blinking my eyes, keeping them closed longer and longer. I started to doze, and suddenly she prodded me. I didn't forget for one moment where I was. My senses were sharpened, heightened.

Silence.

Footsteps? Slow, shuffling, accompanied by heavy breathing.

Three figures appeared in the clearing. I recognised Nikolaj first by the shining of the rims of his glasses. I strained my eyes and thought I saw Marija and Ivan with him. They were leaning on each other, both almost completely worn out. A sweaty bald patch was shining in the moonlight, and Marija tried to breathe silently, but she couldn't help rasping.

They shook hands, and Nikolaj was pointing across the clearing where the hill went downwards. He gave the two rucksacks he had carried on his shoulders to the figures and the old couple added them to their baggage. They shook hands once more, they were in a hurry. The winners went into the forest and the night swallowed them. I was staring into the darkness when I realised Nikolaj was gone.

We waited.

After a long time, Zora started to move slowly. I wanted to cry out with pain as blood shot into my legs again. I almost pushed a rock down the hillside. She grabbed my hand in panic, and we slowly limped down into the valley, hand in hand.

Behind the bunker, the sky was glowing with a metallic hue.

'You understand now?' she asked me.

I told the truth:

'No.'

It seemed she was expecting my answer.

'What did you see?'

'Nikolaj . . .'

'Yes?'

'And the pensioners from 12 Courier Tinček Street . . .'

'Yes?'

'He took them across the border. An illegal crossing.'

'That's right. How I need a cigarette. A coffee. A shower.' She started listing her needs.

'But why?' I finally said.

'They went to claim the jackpot.'

'To the top of the hill?'

'Where are the headquarters of the German Lottery?'

'At your place.'

'Do you remember what the letter said?'

'That they should claim the million in person in fourteen days at the German Lottery headquarters.'

'Yes, but what did it say at the top of the page?'

'Deutsche Lotterie, PF 1512, Berlin, Deutschland.'

She watched me.

'The German Lottery headquarters are in Berlin?' I said, and felt my subthoughts going wild.

She didn't answer.

'Comrades pensioners went to Berlin?'

She nodded.

'Nikolaj took them across the border?'

'Yes.'

Now her words started coming quickly, like in a downpour.

'In return for the safe passage, he got their house and everything in it. He took them to the border, and he arranged for someone to meet them on the other side with a train ticket to Berlin. Tomorrow afternoon Nikolaj leaves for Ljubljana, to take care of the formalities and sell the house to one of the engineers who got a job at the factory.'

I gaped. 'But . . .'

She waited.

'Our headquarters are here' – I pointed with my finger. 'Not there' – I swung my hand in the direction, probably wrong, of Berlin.

'Yes, there's nothing there,' she said icily.

'Nothing?'

'You know very well there's nothing.'

'But Marija and Ivan are going to go to Berlin searching for the German Lottery . . . They won't find it.'

'Because it isn't there. Because it's us.'

'What a trip! In vain! How angry they're going to be when they come back!'

'You think?'

'I'd be!'

'Probably they've got some money stashed away and they can buy a return ticket. But how are they going to find a man who will take them back to the top of the mountain? And another man to take them down to the valley? That costs a lot. It costs a house, and they don't have their house now.'

'But . . . Then, they'll stay there!'

'Yes, or try to return on their own. I hope they don't, because our border guards shoot at anything that moves. They're jumpy. And there are mines in some places.'

'They'll stay there?'

'Yes, probably in a refugee camp. They're without relatives, old. They've got no place to go. There comes an age when you can't start your life over again.'

I could hardly breathe, though my mouth was completely open. 'Nikolaj has done this? Nikolaj?'

'Yes, my husband. I hardly know him any more.'

She dropped her shoulders and bowed her head.

'My husband. The idea has changed him. He's not the same. I don't even know if he's still human. He turned the humanitarian German Lottery into a death machine that's going to make a fortune for him.'

'It will?'

'Toni, don't be naïve. He told me himself the rules had changed. He gave you two hundred letters because he wants to pay out two jackpots each week. The engineers need the houses.'

I took my head in my hands.

'Yes, I didn't believe it at first either. You're married to a person and you think you know them. But then money comes in between. I wanted you to see with your own eyes what became of my husband. You wouldn't have believed me otherwise, and I couldn't blame you.'

I wailed and bolted.

She called after me, but I was too quick. Nikolaj's silver-rimmed glasses and the image of two old figures with bent backs disappearing into the night, into darkness, appeared before my eyes. Now they were on a train headed for Berlin, looking forward to the wealth, happiness, contentment, and Nikolaj was already selling their house.

I couldn't wind up the bell. I banged on the door.

It opened. I wanted to scream that he was a murderer, but he hit me so hard with his walking stick that I fell and probably lost consciousness for a moment. I suddenly found myself sitting on the porch with my legs wide apart, holding my forehead, blood oozing between my fingers.

You see, I still have the scar. Here it is.

'Go in,' he said in a completely calm voice.

It didn't even cross my mind he could hit me again or even kill me. I stumbled into the room and fell into the chair.

'What's wrong with you?' he said.

'I've seen you – you murderer! Berlin, the retired comrades . . .'

'You've seen me? How?'

I realised I was putting Zora in danger. It wouldn't be wise for me to reveal there were two witnesses to the illegal crossing.

'I was wondering how you were going to pay out the million. I followed you . . .'

'What do you know? The kid is smarter than we thought. All right. What now?'

'They have to get the house back!'

'Impossible. I'm selling it and coming back with the papers for the new owners on Tuesday.'

'They have to!'

He slapped his stick against his palm. 'Don't be a fool.'

I went quiet.

'Listen to me, Toni. What's done is done. Even the communists had amnesty. Why shouldn't the German Lottery? So, you don't want us to pay out any more jackpots?'

'No.'

'Have I hit you too hard, or can you follow me? Imagine you're seventy or eighty – in a word, you're old. You've got no one, you're all alone. There's nobody to leave something to. No one to work for. The state gives you food stamps, perhaps a pension. It's not much, but you don't need more. You've got a roof over your head, an entire house. It keeps you nice and cool in summer and warm in winter. You're not missing anything. Then, you get a letter that says you can get a million marks in faraway Berlin, if you trade everything you own for something you don't need. What would you do with a million, if you were in their place? Buy a bigger house? Keep cooler in the summer and warmer in the winter? Buy youth?

'You see, this is how you have to view the German Lottery: it's a tool for seeking out weak people. Greedy, grabby, mean. We seek them out and export them to Germany. And our young country gets better and cleaner with every export. Do you remember the letters from the ones who turned us down? Upright and noble people? Let them stay here. We need them. But there's no harm in losing those who've left.

'Toni, I have to catch a train. I've got a meeting in Ljubljana. I've got to shave and get ready. Please, think about it till Tuesday. The German Lottery is not about money. It's about virtues. It helps us separate the moral wheat from the chaff. I know you're among the former. You've never asked for any payment, not once.

'Have you ever stolen any winnings?'

I shook my head.

'Well, you see? But you could have. You've had every chance. Why shouldn't only honest people like us stay in this country?

'The train doesn't wait for anyone. I've got to go.'

I found myself on the veranda, not knowing when he'd given me the handkerchief I was holding over my head wound.

Zora was leaning on the fence, looking at me. She shuddered as if a bad memory had crossed her mind and then went past me into the house without a greeting.

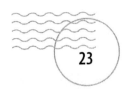

23

No, of course the German Lottery wouldn't work today. You've got to have closed borders, an isolated country, troops on the alert. But sadly there are always countries like that in the world.

Back at work, I told them I'd fallen, not that anybody was terribly interested.

Marija and Ivan disappearing into the night. The leaves swallowing them. Darkness. Gloom. I couldn't get that image out of my mind.

It was like my childhood disappearing – my childhood the way it was supposed to be.

But these two people, this perfect couple, full of calmness and warmth, the way their eyes met, their self-sufficiency – was that just a façade? Was I only imagining all of it? Were they completely different than the way I saw them? I was filled with terrible anger that made me sink my fingers into the bag, squeezing it like it was a neck. The greedy bums, how they fooled me! Sitting there, not wanting anything out of this world, giving me a few minutes a day, and then a million marks comes along and they drop everything, including me. Nikolaj was right. What business did an old woman with a garden and an old man with a pension have in Berlin? They were grabby, greedy! He was right, I kept saying to myself. Right. They betrayed me.

But, can we be the ones who test liars? Can we judge them? Profit from them? Can we cast the first stone? My mother's upbringing came back to me.

At that very moment, Nikolaj was in Ljubljana, selling a house that wasn't his. It was legal, but not moral.

How long did the journey to Berlin take? They were still on the train, full of hope and happiness.

When I went past their house, the windows shut, the carnations watered to the point that the water was brimming over, I almost cried.

It was me, my actions, that emptied that house! I changed two destinies! It was horrible, but somewhere in my sub-thoughts I also found it fascinating.

Zora was waiting for me on the veranda.

'We've got to talk.'

I sat down and the bag hung heavily from my shoulder. I took it off absentmindedly.

I saw she didn't know how to begin. She had to tell me something hard, unpleasant. Perhaps I could just walk away and pretend I was a regular postman who didn't know her and didn't have anything to do with the German Lottery. A nice thought, but completely useless. Childish.

Something's just occurred to me. I don't know if I'll be able to express it. Look, I'm seventy-seven. And you'd think all my thoughts would be as old as I am. But they're not! It's as if for every year of our lives a little piece is left inside us and its thoughts remain the same age. So I have thoughts of a twenty-year-old, a thirty-year-old, a seven-year-old – you see?

111

Well, it doesn't matter.

Where was I? Ah, Zora getting ready.

In addition to the cup she was holding in her hands, there were two more on the tray, empty. She really didn't want to miss me.

'Nikolaj is my husband. Whatever you may think of me, I'm faithful to him.'

She waited for my blushing to go away.

'I stand by his side. But how much longer can I? The lottery? A hundred winners? Against my will, but OK! Those two pensioners who left for Berlin yesterday? Maybe, maybe. But . . . Before he left he proposed something I can't be a part of. Because his proposal goes against my moral core.'

You see, that was the first time I heard the expression. There are words that bring beauty with them, even though they're made up just from sounds, like all others. *Moral core* is like that.

She crushed the empty cigarette box and started fumbling nervously among the books and papers, until she found another one that had already been opened. The cigarette butt began to curve because she held it so firmly in her lips. After each puff, she picked little bits of tobacco from her lips with her tongue and spat them into the corner.

She leaned forward.

It was only when I started coughing that I realised I was copying her, taking in a deep breath, expecting her scent. I only breathed in the smoke.

She waited and crushed her cigarette into a full ashtray.

We gazed at each other.

'Maybe you'll have to be killed.'

I heard her, but I didn't understand.

'Eh?'

'That's what he said.'

'Nikolaj? Who? Why?'

'You, Toni. You. Nikolaj is the victim of the idea, and it's going to get worse. Especially because he's had a taste of the money. If you breathe in a lot of air, you get dizzy. If you drink a lot of water, your stomach bursts. If you get a lot of money, you become a different person. Two hundred letters. Two winners a week. That's a lot of money.'

'But he – he's a writer, he's got . . . '

'He hasn't written anything for a long time now. He doesn't have that much . . . Think about it. Two houses a week. For now. Later, maybe three, four – more and more. He's not going to stop. He's entered a world without any rules, and he hasn't got the inner strength to control himself, so he'll have to be stopped.'

'What about me?'

'You know his secret. If he kills you, a new postman will come along and perhaps he'll cooperate in the lottery. For money! You work because of your belief, and so you remind Nikolaj all the time of the moral core he has lost. If you notify the police, we all go to jail.'

'But I –'

'Yes, please don't tell the police, because Nikolaj could even be sentenced to death, and we could face long years in jail. We'll get out when we're old, if ever. You won't tell, will you?'

'No.'

'You promise?'

'I promise. It's not our fault! It's his –'

'They won't believe us. The German Lottery is the three of us. Who'd believe it wasn't planned this way from the beginning?'

'But it wasn't!'

'Only each of us knows the truth. Think about it.'

She moved away.

I found it difficult to breathe. My left ear was buzzing with fear, my head was ringing, and I desperately needed to go to the toilet.

'Maybe I'll have to be killed too,' she said.

'Eh?'

'No, he didn't say it, to be fair. Perhaps he just slightly hinted at it. Or I'm too scared and I just imagined it. If you have a good idea on the one hand, and a wife and a post-man who are getting in your way on the other, the choice isn't difficult. There are many women and postmen in the world, but only one idea!

'Go now, before a neighbour comes along. Having coffee with a postman is normal, but I don't want to start any rumours. Go!'

She had to tell me a few more times before I picked up my bag. I took the first couple of steps, and then I bolted for the forest and crouched down among the coltsfoot leaves. Everything spilled out of me, upstairs and downstairs, and I thought it would never stop.

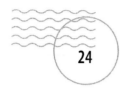

24

I was practising fighting poses in my bathroom in front of the mirror, but I wasn't very good at it. Partly because I still had the runs and had to sit on the toilet, but also because the other residents were returning from work and banging on the door.

I knew I wouldn't be able to go to sleep, so I didn't bother lying down. I sat on my bed, wiping off my sweat. Suddenly, I caught myself sliding down and was glad, thinking I might fall asleep after all, but of course I didn't. The gladness drove away the sleepiness. I lay on my back, looking at the ceiling, at the moving shadows of the passers-by. The newcomers from the south brought a strange custom with them. They would go for a walk before sleep. Back home they probably walked by the sea and met their friends, while here they walked along the road, greeting strangers. There was a shout here and there, they laughed, but I was just scared.

I had a feeling the bed was going to disappear from underneath me and I'd start falling. The floor wouldn't stop me, because it wouldn't be there any more. I still remember the feeling vividly, but I don't know what it meant. Maybe it took hold of me because I was hanging in some sort of limbo, the way I see it now. First I believed in my mother's martyrs, then in socialist secretaries, and finally in the German Lottery. That night, I started losing my faith and foundation. In my rounds, I saw all kinds of things that kept people going: reasoning, love, sacrifice, work. Me, I'm a believer. If I don't believe in somebody or something, I start losing my footing.

My past feelings returned. The fear that I'd done something wrong, that my brothers would wake me up and kick me around. The fear that my father would forget me when passing out the food, which sometimes happened. The fear that the world would end. So many fears. How many could fit into such a weak body in any case? But it's a tall body; maybe fears are stacked one on top of the other, like compost.

I started counting them. After the three I just mentioned, there was the fourth one: I'd be thrown out of my home. The fifth: I wouldn't have a place to sleep. The sixth: I'd lose my job. The seventh: I'd become very ill and be a burden to others. The eighth . . .

I was counting and counting and fell asleep.

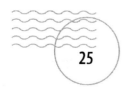

25

The alarm clock woke me up. I jumped to my feet and ran to the bathroom. I was peeing, despite everything that spilled out of me the day before. I thought it was strange that there was no queue and that the home for singles was quiet.

Then I remembered it was Sunday, but I couldn't recall when I had set the alarm clock unawares.

The other day I told you good things about the alarm clock, but now I have to add there is nothing worse than having the meaning that has just been given to you taken away.

On Sunday, there was no work to drive away my fears with routine.

Even if I went to the post office, it would be locked, and only the manager had the key. And what would I do there?

Could Nikolaj really kill me?

His eyes, how they blazed! With an inhuman glow!

Human nature! Hardly five years after unimaginable millions of people had been killed, killings still went on, just more slowly, and I was asking myself if it could happen to me too. Funny, the older I get, the less I fear death. Probably because I've lived so long, and my experience tells me it's less likely to happen. What nonsense!

Maybe Zora was hearing things, was feverish?

I had to see her.

I didn't dare ring the bell – I thought it was inappropriate – so I knocked lightly, but she heard all the same.

She looked left and right and pulled me into the room.

'How glad I am you've come!'

She held me by the elbows and kissed me on the cheeks.

Her warmth, her scent, more coffee and cigarettes this time. I became dizzy.

'Come, sit.'

She took me to a chair and sat me down like I was a helpless invalid.

She sat down at the other end of the table, moved the chair up, and our knees touched. She was too excited to notice.

'Toni, forgive me . . . Yesterday, I tried imagining you were gone . . . I went to the shop, bought something, had a fight with the cashier over the food stamp, went back, cooked, smoked, drank coffee and more coffee, lit up one cigarette after another, and kept telling myself Toni was gone. Gone. Toni. But I knew all along you weren't. It was unimaginable, you being gone. You're special. Please don't think anything bad, indecent. You're the purest creature, so precious. You've got to be. You've got to! Please be. Please, for me!'

I took her hands in mine and she held on to me.

'I will! I will!'

'Really? Will you really?'

'Yes.' I nodded. 'Yes!'

She pulled me to her and put her arms around me. It was

118

worse than the time we were hanging the washing, but not as bad as the time she was in my room.

I remember her scent even today – that blend through which you seem to swim to the surface of a mountain lake. Have you ever tried it? Go as deep as possible and it will feel as if you're frozen – you'll feel ice in your bones. Then you swim up, and the first clouds of warmth go over you – in her case coffee and cigarettes – then the tepid layer, the perfume. And finally, the water on the surface, warmed by the sun. Each person has a different scent. Her scent, how I miss it. How I miss it!

I shouldn't evoke it. The one thing I shouldn't evoke. Her scent, her scent!

Thank you. The wastebasket's over there. Have you got any more tissues?

Suddenly she moved away and looked at me in a strange way. 'Let him kill me, not you!'

'No!' I jumped up. 'He's not going to kill anyone!'

I stood before her, and she watched me like a statue of a saint. She even brought her arms to her chest.

'No one!' I assured her again.

She got up. 'What will you do?'

'Err . . . I don't know. I won't give you up. I won't give in!'

She put her hand on my shoulder. I turned my cheek to her, but she just kept looking at me for a long time.

'Toni, I don't know if this is wise . . .'

She went over to the cupboard, opened the top drawer, and came back with a bundle wrapped in red canvas. She unwrapped it and held a German army pistol in her hand.

'Toni, you've got to promise me. I don't want to have

anything on my conscience. I don't want to regret this. Only in self-defence. Right?'

'Right.'

'Really?'

I reached for the weapon.

She moved it away. 'You swear?'

I swore and took the gun.

She studied me with a serious expression on her face. I knew she was wondering if she'd done the right thing. I didn't want to let her down, so I threw out my chest and lifted my chin.

I put the gun in my pocket.

'I'll protect you, you're safe,' I assured her once more at the door.

'Toni, thank you. I knew I could count on you.' She added, 'The safety catch is on the side. You have to switch it before you shoot.'

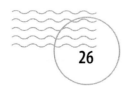

26

You're interested, eh? Ha, ha. Now you've started visiting me every day. When you leave and see the others in the TV room, think – could they all have stories as interesting as mine? Maybe even more? We're not just shrivelled sacks of bones, you know. At least, not all of us.

Something to sign again? How many pages again? The bureaucracy! Glasses . . . Oh, come on, show me. Where? Telling a story is like an avalanche. The first few stones start rolling with difficulty, but then it bursts. Here, it's signed, and you know where the identity card is.

That's how I got a gun. I became a hero in my bathroom. I was pulling the gun from my pocket in a manly way, looking at the imagined opponent from under my brow. I couldn't imagine Nikolaj. I practised drawing, found the safety catch and switched it. I wasn't completely inexperienced. We had military drills in the home for war orphans – rifle practice.

But in my room, I started having doubts. The gun lay on my nightstand and it seemed out of place. It didn't belong there; it wasn't a part of me. It occurred to me somebody could come in, so I put it under the pillow. During the night, I kept checking to see if it was still there, and I was afraid I would shoot myself in my sleep.

But I did feel safer with the gun than without it, I have to admit.

In the morning I opened my eyes even before the alarm clock went off. I lay waiting for the ringing and looking at the ceiling. It was summer. I heard the birds twittering and the metal parts of machines in the factory yawning; they were never turned off. I wasn't completely awake; my eyelids were closing, stopping, opening again. My uniform was on the hanger, the peak of the cap shining in the crystal light.

I'm a postman.

Postmen don't kill with guns, but with letters.

My eyelids were closing, the thought was disappearing.

I froze.

Postmen don't kill with guns, but with letters.

A strange feeling started growing in the pit of my stomach, some sort of tingling. It started spreading upwards, pouring into my head, and it finally woke me up. We exist only in the present, despite the fact we always think about the past and make plans for the future, but at that moment I really landed in the present. It was a unique feeling I'd never had before.

Postmen don't kill with guns, but with letters.

I didn't dare move. I didn't want the tingling to go away, but it was already melting away in my body, leaving me.

Postmen . . .

It's going to disappear!

I jumped to my feet and looked at myself. I seemed quite ordinary – the spindly legs in the pajama bottoms, the bare chest, the arms that had become a bit stronger because of the mailbag.

But something extraordinary was going on inside me.

I tried to bring back the feeling, but I couldn't. However, I knew what had happened.

I'd had an idea!

I! Who was despised at home and called unfit for military service in the home for war orphans. I, whom Nikolaj wanted to get rid of, had just had an idea!

But . . .

Errr . . .

What on earth did it mean?

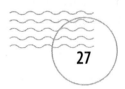

27

I smuggled the gun to work and put it in my bag. It was rattling until I stuffed some letters around it. I had more and more doubts that I'd be able to use it. You see:

Postmen don't kill with guns, but with letters.

Whenever I whispered that statement to myself, it rang magically within me. I was hammering it like a stake into my inner darkness, letting it bring the light in; every whisper brought a better view. Tissue started weaving around it, flesh growing, bones straightening.

You must have heard the growth of an idea being compared with the growth of a child, and it really is similar.

When going over the bridge, I finally realised what I had to do.

Up to the moment when I started winding up Zora's doorbell, I wanted to tell her about the idea, because it seemed so great that I was brimming with excitement and could hardly keep my mouth shut. But when I saw her frightened face, the dark circles under her eyes, the cigarette between her trembling fingers, it struck me. I couldn't do it. Her husband, whom she had known for many years, had changed. I, whom she'd been meeting only for a few months, thinking I never had an idea, had just had one. I wasn't who I seemed to be. The poor thing. How wrong she was about people. Some people just don't have insight. I didn't say anything, out of pity. Later, of course, also because I wasn't too sure that the idea was really that great.

But I assured her confidently that she was safe. I was and would be taking care of her as long as she wanted me to. The trace of the idea must have marked my voice, because she watched me with surprise, trying to decide whether she could trust me. After all, she was just a helpless woman.

She even asked me, 'Was it the gun that changed you?'

I had to really think about what she was saying.

'Of course. Will you make me a cup of coffee, please?'

She stared at me in amazement.

'You really have changed!'

When she left for the kitchen, I quickly grabbed some stamped German Lottery envelopes and tossed them into my bag.

I was in a hurry so I burnt my mouth with coffee. I had to run into the coltsfoot leaves again. I really can't stand coffee. Or was it just nerves?

Looking back, I think I was right not to tell Zora about the birth of my idea. Ideas have the power to pull a man away from a woman, so women have every reason not to like them.

I never had another idea, so don't be angry with me if I say it again:

Postmen don't kill with guns, but with letters.

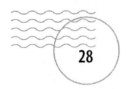

28

I took the envelopes on Monday, and Nikolaj was coming back on Tuesday evening, on the last train.

I wasn't picturing him dead, just out of the way. They'd come, take him away, and he'd be somewhere else, where he wasn't a threat to me or Zora. He could reflect on everything in peace, forget the German Lottery and become a writer again, like he once was. Someone who didn't care about money and liked to give it away to others.

Zora was worried too. In the evening she was tossing pebbles into my window, but the workers who were taking a walk noticed her and scared her away with whistles before I was able to run down to the street.

I caught up with her at the beginning of my delivery route and walked her home.

She also had a plan.

'Please, come tomorrow. Let's wait for Nikolaj together. He won't just shoot us. He can't have changed that much. But I called him this afternoon from the post office and he sounded strange, very strange . . . Feel this. I still have goosebumps.'

She really did.

'I'm afraid, Toni, you're my only hope!'

I kept telling her not to worry, that everything would be

all right. Of course I would go and wait with her.

The poor thing was so scared she wanted to huddle up to me, like I used to huddle up to cows in my childhood. But I became obsessed with my idea too, so I left her before midnight and ran back to the home for singles. I had to wait for the doorman to go on a round before I could creep back to my room.

Three letters. That would do.

I took the empty envelopes and opened them.

I carefully wrote Nikolaj's address in block letters and wiped the letter off a few times with my pyjama top because of the fingerprints.

I took three letters from the pile I kept hidden under my nightstand – those were the letters to winners I didn't deliver during Nikolaj's absence – and opened them. I only put the sheets of paper that had results on them on the table, looked at the columns of figures, and kept wiping off fingerprints for a while. Then I wrapped my pyjama top around my fingers and somehow managed to put the sheets into the envelopes addressed to Nikolaj.

I sealed them and gazed at my creation: the letters of the German Lottery from Berlin, addressed to Nikolaj Klemenc, containing nothing but sheets with the results. Figures, figures, and more figures.

Perhaps they were only looking for spies in Ljubljana, and not in small towns.

The three letters seemed like three postal bullets.

In the morning, I put one of them in the rack and waited. After a minute, I pulled it out a bit, so the manager couldn't overlook it. A moment later I thought that was overdoing it, so I pushed it back in.

And out again.

Remembered fingerprints and broke out in sweat.

Remembered my job. A postman's fingerprints must be on the outside of letters.

Out again. In again.

It wasn't before the manager appeared that I stopped moving it. If he had looked at me, I would have immediately told him everything, but he faced the rack as soon as he walked in through the door. He slowly went over the piles, the letters were bending under his finger, rustling. He smoothed his hair with his left hand . . .

And skipped the German Lottery letter.

He evened out the little pile of letters he took out by tapping them on the table and then turned to leave.

'Excuse me . . .'

He didn't hear me!

'Comrade manager!'

'Yes?'

'This letter – perhaps it's a bit . . . perhaps a bit strange.'

I pointed at it with the tip of my index finger.

His fingers started moving.

I just stared at them as they wiggled without pause.

'Well, give it to me, comrade postman!'

I pulled the envelope out of the rack and gave it to him. As soon as he saw the stamp, his eyes narrowed.

'Hmm,' he murmured and left.

I had to wait for a drop of sweat to fall from my sideburn, trickle down to my earlobe, run around it, and fall on my shoulder, before I was able to take a breath.

An idea is a strange thing. When I was thinking about how to explain it to you, I thought of vegetables, of plants.

After all, I grew up on a farm. You see, you throw everything into the soil. What else is soil but remains – remains
upon remains? And then a seed is planted, and it will grow
only if it has everything it needs. If something's missing,
forget about it. This is how I wanted to explain it to you,
but now I see that even I don't understand it, or I've forgotten. It doesn't matter.

Look. Do you remember when I talked about that Mr
Comrade Minister who gave a speech about how they discovered spies that were corresponding in code? It was even
in the papers. I heard it, and it didn't mean anything at
the time. It fell into me like a little drop of water into soil
and remained there. And then I had an idea, and the idea
needed that little drop of spy-hunting for it to grow.

My idea was to start sending Nikolaj his own results in
the German Lottery envelopes. Eight columns of figures,
different in each letter. All the letters from a hostile country! From the imperialist West. In those times, comrades
in long black coats came to get you for a bad joke in a bar,
let alone for a good one! In the evening, you were laugh-
ing in the bar; the next morning, you were already crying before an interrogator. So I thought they were bound
to discover some code if they looked at all those figures.
Mathematicians are geniuses, which means they can't look
at eight columns of random figures and not find some hidden meaning in them.

They would come for Nikolaj and take him away.

My first and only idea.

The only problem was, nothing happened.

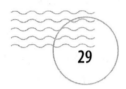

29

An idea takes you apart and puts you back together again in a slightly different way than you've been built before. And then you go thinking the world has changed too, and it hurts when you discover it didn't change, didn't even notice your idea. No wonder so many people would rather go about changing the world than facing the pain of their disappointment.

I told Zora I was in a hurry and she shouldn't worry, everything was taken care of. She watched me suspiciously. I ran away before she could say anything.

When I was returning from my round, I ran into her in front of the post office.

She stopped only for a moment. 'I spoke with Nikolaj. He's coming back at ten, and he sounded icy cold. Will you stand by me?'

'I will.'

Then she added in a softer voice, 'Thank you. Come at nine.'

I was taking my time at the post office, rummaging around the rack, hoping the comrades in long black coats would pick up Nikolaj in Ljubljana and my idea would work immediately, like magic.

It's just struck me that I didn't know anything about the

manager. He seemed distant and terrible, with his moustache and stony gaze. Maybe he only pretended to be tough because he wanted to get through hard times by causing as little suffering as possible.

I didn't think about that back then, of course. In the evening, I put the remaining two letters among the collected mail and knocked on his door. He put them down in front of him and sent me off without opening them. A vein in his temple was throbbing.

I was growing stranger by the minute. As if I were moving away from myself. Try it. Close your eyes, and you'll have a feeling you're in the centre, right? Well, I moved to the right. No, I don't mean politically. It's just that I felt as if I were walking next to myself, like there were two of us, and I was watching myself.

I took the gun and went to Zora's.

Didn't you say you had to go to college?

Ha, ha.

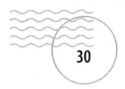

30

She locked the door twice behind me and bolted it.

'Have you got the gun?'

I showed it to her.

'The safety catch?'

'Off.'

'You haven't forgotten what you promised?'

'Only in self-defence.'

'Yes, I don't want any blood. Maybe we can make him come to his senses by talking to him. But . . . how do you know somebody's lying, especially if they're convincing? And when you turn your back, they stab you from behind. Let's go into the room.'

It was the first time I had entered their bedroom, which was just as richly furnished as the luxurious writer's room. Through the window I saw the road up to the bend, a part of the forest, and over it, a reddening sky where the sun, invisible to me, was setting, taking its leave from the mountains. I still stood there, torn and calm.

'Sit.'

She gestured toward the bed.

She sat next to me. 'Maybe it's not proper to bring you here, but I like this view. It's the only view from this house that calms me down.'

We watched the mountains together. The highest peaks were still capped in snow.

'They don't seem quite real, especially in the summer, when it's hot in the valley. Like a mirage – you know what that is?'

'No.'

'It's something you see in the desert, but it's not there. Like –'

'A ghost?'

'Yes, like a ghost. Only it's not invented. It's just not where everybody is looking, but somewhere else. When I was little, I liked reading adventure books most of all – boys' books, travels over the desert, caravans, adventures, Karl May, Sienkiewicz. Have you ever read them?'

I shook my head. 'My father didn't like books. He thought it was a mortal sin if someone was making something up instead of working.'

I remembered my mother's religious magazines he wanted to use to light a fire, but he wasn't allowed to, because the word of God was printed on them. It was the only thing they argued about. Well, they didn't talk much otherwise.

'Is he still alive?'

'No.'

'How did he die?'

'A plane crashed down on him.'

'He was killed by one of the most adventurous ideas of all time. Do you know who invented that plane?'

I shook my head.

'You see, that's what I find most exciting. A working idea, author unknown. That person can watch the planes and knows he put them up there, and he is warmed by the feeling of carrying a secret inside him. How I envy him. I dreamed of flying. I still do! Would you fly with me?'

'I don't know if I'm up for it. I'm a postman.'

She laughed and ruffled my hair. 'And a fine-looking postman at that. Wild hair suits you!'

She left me alone until I stopped blushing.

'Aren't you hot?'

It really became stuffy. A fly was knocking against two window panes, trapped. A bee buzzed past the window now and again.

'Take off your jacket. It's summer!'

I did as she said.

She undid the top button on my shirt.

'My memory is right. You're not hairy.'

I moved away. And I could only move towards the middle of the bed.

'It's hot. I'm nervous.'

She was caressing my shoulders as if she were ironing the sleeves of my shirt.

'You've got such gentle and fine arms, like porcelain.'

Her finger got caught against a button on my shirt and tore it off. She kept apologising and opened the fabric to see if she'd damaged it.

'How your heart is pounding!'

She checked it with her whole hand and caught my nipple between her index and middle finger.

'You're hot!'

She undid another button.

'Please, don't!'

'Don't worry.' She looked into my eyes up close, slightly

134

above me, as if trying to catch her reflection in them. 'I know what I'm doing.'

I was blushing and getting lost in her scent. It seemed even stronger than usual, not only because of the perfume, also because of the stuffy air in the room. Her body was steaming, glowing. Wafts from her cleavage were hitting me, wet, sweltering and inviting.

She traced her finger over my lips.

I tried to push her hand away, but I was spent, powerless, as if all blood had been drained from my limbs. My arm fell and landed on her thigh.

'Ouch, you animal,' she whispered.

I was about to faint. Zora was moving up and away, swirling and coming into focus. Her tongue was between her lips, moistening them, moving slowly to the corners, stopping, drawing back into her mouth, touching the tips of her teeth on the way.

Right there, at that moment, the world should have stopped. Frozen and remained captured. That would have been heaven. That was the only thing I was capable of thinking about, and I'll sign that any day!

Zora was the first to hear the steps.

'He's coming!'

Who, what, when? I was turning my head, completely at a loss.

'Shhh!' She nudged me in the direction of the window.

Nikolaj's figure in an undone raincoat stepped from the road and started walking along the path. He was carrying a small wicker case in his right hand. Pebbles were flying from under his feet.

I must have made a loud moan, because she placed her

hand over my mouth and told me again to be quiet. 'Have you got the gun?'

I took the weapon and pointed it at the window.

'Only in self-defence, you swore!'

I was probably calm up to that moment because I thought Nikolaj would never come. I had blind trust in the state and its men in long black leather coats. But the authorities hadn't done anything – the man who wanted to kill me was coming!

'He's mad,' she whispered. 'I know it from his pace. Livid! Look. Do you see?'

I stared, and his walk really seemed wild.

He disappeared from view.

We heard him step on the veranda and ring.

I flinched. Zora put her arms around me and drew closer.

Nikolaj started to knock.

He put the key in the lock and turned it twice.

He tried to open the door.

The bolt!

He rang again, banged. Then there were steps.

I secretly looked at Zora, who was staring through the window. She seemed completely calm, but watchful. I was sweating, trembling, trying to get the drops of sweat out of my eyes by blinking. She held me with both arms, as if trying to keep me back, though I didn't want to move.

There was strange scratching and groaning, right under the window.

The woodpile! He'd got onto the woodpile from the veranda and was making his way to the window.

The sun had already set, and the last hues of the day

were hanging over the mountains. The dusk was growing denser.

Nikolaj's figure sprang up, banging against the window, the wood shaking under his feet. The window started to open. Zora, poor girl, had forgotten to bolt it in her distress. The window ledge went up to his waist; he gripped it. The white triangle of the handkerchief in his breast pocket was shining in the evening light. Zora still had her arms around me.

Nikolaj put his hand through the opening and pushed the right side of the window. Then he looked down . . .

'He's got a gun!' Zora whispered.

I saw it in his hands.

Funny, how memories work. Funny. Sometimes they aren't quite right. Now that I'm telling you this, I can see him clearly, and it seems to me he didn't have anything in his hands a moment earlier, and then suddenly there was a gun. As if he'd found it there, on the ledge, had looked at it in surprise. But it doesn't make any sense! How memories toy with us. How distorted they become.

He opened the left side of the window, too, and threw his leg over the ledge. He was waving the gun, trying not to lose his balance.

Suddenly Zora wasn't there with me.

She was standing at the door, and she turned on the light.

'He'll kill you, Toni! Shoot! Shoot!'

Nikolaj was leaning through the window, his legs astride the sill, blinking. I stood up and pointed the gun at him.

Zora was screaming he would kill me.

The gun was invented for the same reason as every other

device – to make our work easier. I can't imagine strangling a man. It must take time and strength. And most importantly, you have to look at him, endure the agony of his death. That's why a knife was invented. Quicker, but still close up. A gun is just a trigger you pull.

But I couldn't handle even that. I couldn't.

Nikolaj raised the hand in which he held the gun, automatically – he seemed to be in shock – and lowered it.

I realised I had lowered my hand too, even before him.

We stood there and stared at the floor.

Zora stopped screaming.

She was looking from one to the other, as if choosing.

'So.' He looked at her. 'You're tired of me. Me, who always carried out your ideas. Who always protected you, took everything upon myself. You wanted me to become a writer, and I became one, despite my lack of talent. You wanted the Wise Men's Riddle, and you got one. And I got two years in jail. And then the German Lottery, and you got that too. What else do you want? Have you gone crazy?'

'You've gone crazy! You! Ten, twenty winners at the most! Not a hundred! Not two hundred! Because it all went to your head. You were nobody when I found you. And then you became all high and mighty and started overdoing it!'

'Small! Always keeping it small! So no one would notice! Wouldn't it be better to take the money in one go and enjoy the rest of your life?'

I was caught in the middle of a family quarrel. I could only watch, though I didn't quite know what they were talking about.

'That's the difference between you and me, Nikolaj. That's it – I enjoy the work, I'm not after the money!'

They were screaming at each other, and Nikolaj was waving his hands as if wanting to nail each sentence to the ground. Zora slapped on the door, trying to shut him up.

Darkness at the end of the path, at the bend, but then lights, something long and black gliding down the asphalt.

A car?

Two.

Standing still, not moving.

Nikolaj and Zora were still screaming at each other, but I wasn't listening.

They turned off the headlights; the cars disappeared.

Was there somebody running along the path – not on the gravel, a bit higher up, on the grass, to keep quiet?

Zora . . . Zora was incredible, now that I think about it. In the middle of the fiercest quarrel, she noticed my alertness and obviously saw them too, because I cannot imagine why else she would have stopped her attack in the middle of a sentence and shouted to me:

'Throw him the gun!'

I did as she said, and Nikolaj caught it automatically.

And he went right on with his screaming. He was too furious to stop:

'What's wrong with you two? Why are you giving me these guns? I've never killed anyone, and I'm not going to!'

He was flailing his arms, a weapon in each hand. Once, he almost struck his glasses with a gun barrel, as if he were bothered by the fact that he couldn't check his lenses because his hands were full. His back was to the window, he was lit as though on stage, and the figures of comrades in long black leather coats were entering the circle of light.

Zora sprang and knocked me to the floor.

'What the –' were his last words.

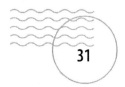

31

I thought I'd have to face the music, but I was lucky. Zora never found out about my idea. We never talked about why the comrades in long black leather coats came at precisely the right time. Once, she mentioned she had anonymously notified the police, just in case. They were very touchy about armed elements back then; you couldn't go brandishing your guns around, not even in your own bedroom. Even now I don't know if my idea worked at all. The manager didn't mention anything, and neither did I.

The comrades didn't ask any questions about the German Lottery; they obviously didn't know about it. They smiled at me, and I saw why when they allowed me to go to the toilet. My shirt was unbuttoned to the waist, my hair ruffled, and there were lipstick marks on my face. It wasn't right they thought so poorly of Zora, but I didn't dare say anything. I was no hero. If I had been, I would have shot Nikolaj myself. I was washing in that smelly toilet and feeling how the spirits of the seven secretaries of SKOJ were leaving me. They fired their guns and died heroic deaths, which I wasn't capable of. As you see, it's true. This old folks' home got me, not a bullet. It was the second time in my life I lost all faith. The bomber took away the saints and the martyrs, and Nikolaj the secretaries. But I wasn't losing my footing now. My thoughts turned to Zora. I sensed a firmness in her that Nikolaj had managed to subdue with his speeches, but he couldn't stifle it.

But a woman like her could have anyone. What did she want with a wretch like me?

They allowed me to see her before I left, and then I went back to the home for singles.

I was sitting on the bed, moaning. Not out of sadness. I was doing the only thing I could think of. It flowed out of me naturally.

I heard whistling. It was getting louder, piercing. The door opened and Zora entered. The doorman was a step behind her, and not knowing what to do, kept repeating, 'Comrade . . . comrade . . .'

She looked at me and pouted. 'Are you coming with me?'

So I went.

That same night the moment arrived when I became a man.

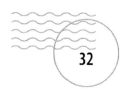

32

No, no, of course I lost my virginity, finally, but that's not what I'm talking about. Anyone can lose virginity; you either put something somewhere or you get something put into you, and that's it. It's easy.

I came against my moral core and learned to say no. That's what I'm talking about.

We were lying in bed. She was tracing her fingers over my chest, this way and that, and sometimes, rarely, she stopped, narrowing her eyes to take a better look at a hair she'd discovered.

She started talking about the future.

I didn't dare ask her if she was satisfied with me, in bed I mean, but when she spoke I was relieved. Satisfied people speak about the future, dissatisfied about the past.

My heart leaped with joy when I realised she wasn't talking just about herself, but about us! We were together, the two of us!

How nicely life takes care of everything. Just when I thought I was alone, forsaken, I found Zora. I didn't miss the martyrs and the secretaries any more.

I can't say she asked me to marry her. In her plans, we were already married. Not that I minded, not at all. I listened to her, and slowly fear started gnawing at me. I knew the moment was coming, the moment I had to tell her, before she started making plans for my profession. I plucked up all my courage and said:

'I'm a postman.'

'I know.'

'And I'll stay a postman. With a bag!'

'I know.'

'You're not mad?'

'Why would I be? Being a postman is a nice and useful profession.'

I listened to her, dozed off for a while, listened again. She didn't stop talking. Her fingers were moving faster and faster. She was getting excited, and then she rested, like a calf that's drunk its fill.

'Darling . . .' she said.

To me! She called me darling!

'Darling, what if we went on with the German Lottery?'

'But do we have the money?'

'Hm, that would be a problem. My parents wouldn't chip in, and we'll hardly get by on your salary alone.'

I thought the subject was closed but she came back to it after a few minutes.

'What if we went on with the lottery the way it was in the end, but with ten winners, only –'

'No.' I tried to stop her.

'Hold on, hold on! And only war criminals get tickets to Berlin, for example. You're a postman, surely you can find bad, evil people who have no relatives on your route – the enemies of the people, collaborators – and we can send them off to claim the jackpots.'

'No. We can't . . . we can't judge . . .'

'From every house we sell, we pay half into a war or-phans' fund?'

'No, it's not –'

'Wait! Even better! We have two German Lotteries. One for the evil people who go to Berlin and leave their houses to us, and the other for the poor, where every ticket wins. We finance the second one from the first one. A great idea. Aren't you excited?'

She pressed me against the bed, and I truly felt trapped. Her closeness, her scent, her body, the memories I had just created were still spinning my head . . . And on the other hand, the pensioners from 12 Courier Tinček Street and the darkness swallowing them. Where were they? Under a tent in a refugee camp? The idea of punishing bad people really sounded attractive. We could make money from it and give aid to those who needed it, but I didn't feel like a judge. If I had been able to judge, I would have pulled that trigger and killed Nikolaj, but I didn't, so I couldn't bring back the German Lottery either.

Her persuasion was hollowing and scooping me out, cut-ting and hacking at me, gnawing me. In the end, it reached my moral core. I felt a firmness inside me that went from my pelvis to my neck; my whole body was supported by it, drawing from it. That strength made me speak, and my voice sounded like never before and never since.

'No.'

Zora went quiet and moved away.

My moral core vanished. Fears of loneliness replaced it. I wanted to apologise, but I didn't dare speak, because I would surely have cried.

We were quiet in the dark.

Then she spoke in a completely normal voice and didn't mention the German Lottery again. Soon she started snuggling up to me again, and she intertwined her plans for the future with compliments that filled me with sweet embarrassment, calling me 'My man!' and 'The man of the new era!'

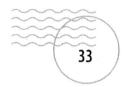

33

Yes, your grandma Zora was a really understanding person. It's a pity she didn't live to see her grandsons, the poor thing. How happy she would have been!

It was hard when we were left without her. Your mother was in secondary school and her brother in his first year of college. Hard. You know neither the day nor the hour, as my mother used to say. But Zora . . . She wanted to fly so badly.

Even before, I was the one who was mostly taking care of the children, I admit, because Zora was a sales representative. First in Yugoslavia, and after the borders opened, all over the world. I remember how excited she was when she came back from her first flight. You sit in a plane like in a bus, but you don't see the pilot, and you have to trust him. She wanted to be a pilot. But they didn't allow women back then . . . Of course not. She took the exam for pilots anyway. Little planes. Her dream was to fly around the world by herself. She was talking about some Amelia. And she went off. It takes many years before they declare someone who disappears over the ocean dead! Here, take this money and please, go and buy some flowers and take them to her grave. I never liked going there. It's a strange feeling, knowing you're standing over nothing but marble. That the woman you loved was divided between thousands and thousands of fish a long time ago.

That's why I don't eat them.

It was an honour being married to her. An honour. It was like being married to Marx, really. Because Zora had even better ideas for humanity than him, and more of them! Smarter too, I'd say. Marx wanted people to give up something for the good of others, while Zora tried to change people for the better through their principal bad trait: greed. They grab and grab, which they would've done anyway, but the beauty of Zora's ideas was they also have to give, which they call investing, and that's how prosperity is built.

But it's true that Zora's and Karl's ideas shared the same fate. Just like communism went bad, so did her ideas. When we needed money for the first TV set, she invented the Wonderful Pyramid, Catch the Cash when we needed the first car, Magic Chain when we had children, and so on. She came up with a nice name for every idea; she thought the idea wasn't complete without it.

Wonderful ideas that would make everybody rich, living in equal prosperity – but Zora remained modest. She invented the idea, I delivered the invitations and letters, and then we stepped back, because others, similar to Nikolaj, stepped in. Blinded by the idea, egotistic, they started hoarding the money for themselves and ruined everything. Until they muscled in, we were doing fine. But all Zora's communisms ended badly, like Karl's did.

Oh, Zora, Zora. What an incurable idealist. Her every idea was snatched away and ruined, but she always invented a new one!

We weren't doing bad financially, even though Zora's parents never got in touch or helped. How many insurance companies Zora had taken out insurance with before she went on her flight! But the letters her attorney brought me were even more important. Each of them contained one of her unused ideas, described down to the last detail, including how far I could go.

So I slowly came by these four houses I'm going to divide equally among my children and grandchildren in my will. Everybody gets the same share. You won't get any less because you're the youngest!

Morals are not something you can get once and for all, you know. You have to keep working on them. When Sarajevo was under siege in 1992, I was tempted to bring back the German Lottery, just for one draw. Sarajevo is a beautiful city. It would be nice to have a holiday house there. But if I could stand up to Zora, I could also stand up to myself.

Now I have nothing but memories. They come back randomly, like snowflakes. I never know which one will come next. I had to catch them and sort them out in the right order to tell you this story. This is all our lives are to others: stories. The brightest memory, the one that keeps flooding back, is the one of Zora sleeping. Before she fell asleep she always cuddled up to me. The deeper her sleep became, the more she moved away. When she was dreaming, she moved to the far end of her side of the bed. Sometimes I woke up at night, and I couldn't take my eyes off her – her face was so different in her sleep from when she was awake. Actually, she wore many faces during the day, but only one at night. And it was the most beautiful one of all, but also strange in a way, because I never saw it in daylight. Maybe I added to it and imagined things. Her, the emptiness of the bed between us, both of us at our own ends of the bed, me not daring to breathe, looking at her, not knowing what she was dreaming about, what she was thinking about. I knew what she told me. That was all. If I had to pick out a single feeling I had when I was around her, it would be the feeling of gratitude that she spent her life with me. A day doesn't go by that I don't feel it.

Pass me a handkerchief, please.

Would the Magic Chain still work?

Well, sure. Everything built on greed is timeless.

I'll tell you tomorrow . . .

Ⓑ *editions*

www.cbeditions.com